Finding Grace

Also by Dawn Renaud:

Plotting for Success: A Step-by-Step Approach to Writing, Editing & Publishing Your Novel

Rain Dance

Finding Grace

Dawn Renaud

[handwritten inscription: Faye— all the best! Dawn Renaud]

D'ÉLAN PUBLISHING

Finding Grace is a work of fiction. Any resemblance to persons living or dead, or to actual events, is purely coincidental. Although some of the communities do exist, they have been re-imagined for this story.

ISBN 978-0-9688583-6-3

Also available in large print 978-0-9938786-2-6, and as an ebook.

Published in Canada by d'Élan Publishing.

Printed in the United States.

The dictionary entries are from Collins Gage Canadian Paperback Dictionary, 2006 edition, published by Thomson Nelson.

This one's for my brothers.

Wednesday, July 25

There's only a bit of light glowing around the edge of the window. Jesse's still in the top bunk, and Macy's trying to wake him up. He grunts. Macy's whisper gets louder. "Come on, Jesse. He's already in a bad mood."

My bed shakes. In the almost-dark, Jesse's legs dangle over the side for a second before he drops to the floor.

Macy's pulled her suitcase out from under her bed and she digs out Mom's scarf and sunglasses, the ones she always takes with her when she has to go with Dad to get the money out of the bank machine. Mom used to wear them sometimes, mostly when she had marks on her face, back when she used to go to town. That was when she could still cook right and help us with our school.

She smelled good, too, and she washed the clothes and everything. At Mosquito Lake, Grace and I would help her hang the washing on the clothesline, and Mom would tell us stories. My favourite was the one about the kids who could fly. I'd imagine Grace and Jesse and Macy and me all flying, zooming across the lake and over the treetops. We'd visit Grandma on our way to Egypt to see the pyramids. Maybe we'd fly past some castles along the way.

Jesse's shaking me. "C'mon," he says. "Mom's already up."

There's more light outside and I open the curtains. The nest in the big evergreen has been empty for a couple of weeks now. I look down the hill past the guest parking lot to the lake. It's dark green this morning, the same colour as the trees that cover the steep bank on the far side. And it's still as glass. The rowboats that are tied to the wharf are barely bobbing.

Smoke's coming out of the chimney at Cabin Three, so we're not the only ones up. A loon call echoes up the lake. It sounds close, but Macy told me that's just the way echoes work. That loon's probably at the end of the lake and there's no point going down to look for it.

I don't know if she's right. I never heard any loons at Mosquito Lake Lodge, where it was all open and swampy and you can see way up the lake, but here at Keneece where the lake is all narrow and twisty and trapped in a steep valley, I hear them every day.

The kettle whistles and I remember I'm supposed to be getting dressed. I put my pajamas under my pillow and make my bed, hurrying so Jesse won't have to call me twice. I stop at the bathroom to pee. It smells damp, like someone had a bath. The tub's been dried and the fan's on, so hopefully the damp smell will be gone by the time Dad gets home.

He and Macy aren't back from town yet, but Mom's already at the table. She's still in her robe. These days she doesn't usually get dressed until after her morning nap, and sometimes she doesn't get dressed at all. Today she's wearing clean pajamas.

"Well, good morning," she says, tugging at the knotted belt of her bathrobe.

"Hi, Mom," I say.

She frowns a little and looks past me, over my shoulder, like maybe someone's there. This is her confused look. "Have you come to visit?" she asks, still working at the knot.

"Yes," I say. "And to make you breakfast."

"What a nice boy you are," she says. "I guess you're big enough to make breakfast. How old are you, about ten or eleven?"

"Just eight," I say, and she makes a frown. "I'm tall for my age."

"Oh," she says. She's undone the knot. "What's your name?"

"Drew," I tell her.

She pulls the belt out of its loops. "Drew," she says, carefully smoothing the belt out on the table. "What the heck kind of a name is that?"

Once in a while, Mom remembers me. Most days she doesn't. Some days, she thinks she has a little baby called Jesse and a toddler called

Macy. Other days she thinks she's still a kid herself and she wants to go to school. This might be
one of those days.

Jesse comes out of Mom and Dad's room with
the garbage bag from the wastebasket and an
armload of bedding. He puts the laundry in the
washing machine and starts it, then heads back
in the bedroom with clean sheets.

I start the toast. Mom usually just has a couple
of pieces with peanut butter and jam. Sometimes
she wants marmalade instead. I hope it won't be
a marmalade day, because we ran out last week.
Maybe Dad and Macy will do some shopping
before they come home. They usually go to
Vernon too early to shop, and the store in
Lumby opens even later. But the freezer's getting
empty. Yesterday I took out the last loaf of bread
and there's been no milk for weeks. I didn't
know whether to tell Dad or not.

Sometimes the guests that come out to rent a
cabin or go fishing don't bring their own food,
and Dad sells some of ours to them. He says if
they are fool enough to pay double the going rate
for cheap-ass food, he isn't going to be fool
enough to hang onto it.

But if any more guests come this week they
better bring their own or they'll be out of luck,
just like us.

I put the strawberry jam and the peanut butter
on the table. Mom's folding her belt into smaller
and smaller rectangles, smoothing and patting it
after each fold. She's humming the song about

three little fishes, the one she used to sing to Grace while she was giving her a bath.

"Breakfast is ready," I say.

She smiles at me. Then she smoothes out her belt along the tabletop and starts folding it again, smaller and smaller and smaller, patting and smoothing, patting and smoothing.

Jesse closes the bedroom door. He picks up the garbage bag and stuffs it into the bin under the sink, and then washes his hands. "Want some coffee, Mom?" he asks. He opens the cupboard where we keep the mugs.

Mom doesn't answer, so he goes around to her side of the table. "Anna," he says. She stops folding and smiles up at him. "Would you like some coffee?"

Mom frowns. "Oh, no," she says, shaking her head. "Coffee's for grownups. I'll have milk."

"We're all out of milk," he says, opening the fridge. "How about some orange juice?"

Mom's eyes narrow. "Are you gonna try to feed me that powdered crap again?"

It's her bad-temper voice, which kind of scares me, but Jesse just smiles at her. "I'm terribly sorry, ma'am. I'd quite forgotten that you don't like our artificial juice. Can I interest you in a nice glass of fresh squeezed water?"

Mom smiles. "Water will do nicely, sir, thank you very much." She takes her belt from the table, wraps it around her waist and ties it, and reaches for the jam.

I keep the toast coming. Jesse has four slices

with peanut butter, and he convinces Mom to eat one whole piece with jam before she takes off her belt and starts folding it again. Jesse moves her water glass and the peanut butter out of her way.

I sit down to have a couple of slices of toast, too, but we're getting low on peanut butter, so I just have mine plain.

Jesse's cleared the table, wiped it, and set up Mom's puzzle. Today's Wednesday, so it's the one with two goldfish in a bowl. I'm just starting to wash the breakfast dishes when there's a knock on the door.

Mom looks up from her puzzle. "Who's there?" she calls. She's made her voice all high-pitched and cheerful like the one she used for the grandmother, back when she read us bed-time stories. I look at the door, half expecting to hear Little Red Riding Hood.

"It's me, Ben Forrester," says the voice from outside.

That's one of the guests' kids. I look at Jesse. We're not supposed to answer the door, but Dad's not here and Mom looks like she's ready to get up and deal with it. Jesse shrugs at me, goes to the front door, pulls his baseball cap off the peg, covers up his hair, and unlocks the dead-bolt. "Hi Ben," he says.

I'm still standing like an idiot with my hands in the sink when Mom starts to get up. "More kids come to visit?" she says.

Jesse steps outside and closes the door behind him.

"Wow, Anna," I say, grabbing the hand towel, "you're doing a great job on that puzzle. Want some help? I think this piece goes here." I fit in a couple of pieces.

It's easy because we've done the same puzzle every Wednesday for almost a year.

Mom glances at the puzzle, but she seems more interested in the door, so I start singing "Three Little Fishes." This is a trick I learned from Macy. Mom usually settles down when you can get her to sing along. Mom looks back at the puzzle. "That one goes over here," she says, grabbing a piece from my hand. "Down in the meadow by an itty bitty pool," she sings, fitting the piece into place.

Jesse's been gone for a while. Mom's already finished the puzzle and we've started it over again. You'd think she'd want to build a new one, but no. She gets upset if you switch them. She just does the same one over and over until nap time. I keep watching the clock, expecting Dad to come busting through the door all mad because Jesse's outside talking to somebody.

It's already after eight-thirty when the door does bust open, but it's only Jesse. His cheeks are red and he's out of breath. He flings his cap onto a peg and comes to help with the puzzle.

"Where were you?" I ask.

"Ben wanted to go for a ride, and his brother was still sleeping," Jesse says.

I can't believe it. "You were out riding a bike?"

Jesse scowls and puts his finger on his lips.

"What if Dad—"

"We rode up the walking trail," he says.

"But what if he came home and you weren't—"

"Macy said they were finally getting some groceries," he says. "Earliest they could be home is nine."

Mom looks at the clock and stands up. "I gotta go now," she says. For a second I think she's decided it's a school day, but she heads for the bathroom instead.

Jesse's still out of breath. He smells like outside, like sunshine. "Man," he says, "that was great."

I put my feet up on my chair seat and pull my knees up to my chin. "Jesse," I say, "do you wish for the old days?"

"Are you crazy?" He tilts his chair way up onto its back legs. "Every single day."

"I've been thinking," I tell him.

"You're always thinking," he says.

I guess that's true. I do think all the time. Doesn't everyone?

"Well?" he says.

"I was thinking we might be able to make Mom okay again."

He snorts, thumping his chair back down. "You found something in Reader's Digest about a cure for strokes?"

I wish. I've been through the musty old pile of magazines over and over. There's stories about Joe's kidneys and Joe's liver and even about stuff that Jane has, too, but there's nothing about their brains. Dad says Mom's stroke made her brain so it can't work right any more.

"I read a story about depression," I say.

Jesse frowns.

I talk fast. "What if Mom didn't have a stroke? What if she was just sad because Dad hit her?" Jesse sucks in his breath and he goes all tense. Crap. I talk faster. "And what if then she got really, really sad because she just misses Grace?"

Jesse looks at me for a long minute, kind of sad or mad, I'm not sure which. Now I wish I'd just let him be happy about his bike ride.

"What do you mean?" he asks.

"Well, a stroke is like a brain injury, right?"

He shrugs. "You're the smart one," he says. Jesse's smart, too. He just means that I'm the one that reads a lot.

"Depression is like being really, really sad," I explain. "The story said researchers think maybe depression can make people act like they had a brain injury."

There's a sound of flushing from the bathroom. "I'm finished," Mom calls, and we can hear her shuffling toward the door. "Oh, wait, maybe not." More shuffling, then the toilet lid clanks open again.

Jesse starts blinking hard, like he does when he's trying not to cry.

"I just want her to be Mom again," I say.

He swallows. "Me too."

So I decide maybe this is a good time to share my great idea. "What if we go find Grace and bring her back?"

I don't know if Jesse's angry or what. "How're we gonna do that?"

"Mosquito Lake Lodge had a guest file just like the one here at Keneece Resort," I say. "We go find out what guests were there the weekend Dad gave her away. Then we call them until we find out who has her."

Jesse looks at the phone. We're not allowed to touch it.

"We can call when Dad's taking care of the guests," I say.

"But when he sees the phone bill, we'll get whupped."

"No we won't." Here's the best part of my plan. "When Mom's okay again, we'll get her to take us home."

Jesse's still frowning. "How do we get to Mosquito Lake?"

"You can drive," I say. "Next time Dad gets drunk—"

"I'm eleven!" he snorts. "Soon as I get on the highway I'd be busted."

Jesse didn't used to be this crabby. "Not if you go at night," I say.

The toilet flushes again. "All done!" Mom calls.

"Please, Jesse," I say. "We'll bring Grace home, and then Mom'll be okay again."

Mom comes skipping out of the bathroom, then stops, scowling. "What are you boys doing here?" she asks.

"We thought you might want to work on this puzzle with us," I say.

Mom still looks angry, so I start singing. "Down in the meadow by an itty bitty pool..."

Mom smiles. "Lived three little fishes and a momma fish, too..." She plops herself into a chair and picks up a puzzle piece.

Jesse looks at me. His eyes are shiny and he's blinking fast. "We'll do it," he says. "But don't tell Macy yet."

"Don't tell her what?" asks Mom.

Jesse looks at her. "It's a surprise," he says.

"Goodie!" says Mom. She starts humming Happy Birthday.

It's after nine now, and I can hear a truck coming down the driveway. It doesn't sound like the lodge truck, though. Jesse gets his cap back on and looks out the window. He looks back at me. There's footsteps coming up the steps and along the porch toward the office window, then the buzzer goes.

"Ding, dong, doorbell," Mom sings out, looking at me, then Jesse. "Well, aren't you going to answer it?"

Jesse takes a big breath, stands up, and goes through the door to the office. I hear the service window slide open.

"Well, hello, sonny. Your dad here?"

The man has one of those fakey voices, like

Mr. Blade, that guy that comes to see Dad twice a month. I glance at the calendar, but no—it's only July 25th. Mr. Blade's not coming until tomorrow.

"Dad's unavailable," says Jesse.

"How about Mom?" the guy asks.

"She's in disposed," Jesse says. Disposed is the code word adults use when someone's really in the bathroom.

"Well, I'll bet you can help me," the guy says. "Me and my lady friend here are looking for a cabin."

"I think we might have one left," says Jesse. Actually, there are four cabins and only one is already rented out. But Jesse's not making up lies. He's just saying what Dad always says. "It's one-fifty, two if you want a boat for the day."

"Nah, we don't—"

"Ooh, a boat!" a woman's voice interrupts, and Mom looks up from her puzzle. "Baby," the woman's voice squeaks. "I never done it in a boat."

Mom looks like she's thinking about going to talk to the guests, so I hand her a puzzle piece and quickly go to close the office door. Through the window I see that the woman on the porch has lots of makeup on, like the models in the magazines but not pretty, and she's got her arms wrapped around a guy in a cowboy shirt. He's holding some money out to Jesse.

"I'm not supposed to handle cash," says Jesse. "Can you wait for my Dad to get back?"

The woman's running her hands up and down

the guy's body. "Oh, honey," she says, and her voice is all weird, like she's pretending to be the big bad wolf. "I don't wanna wait."

I close the office door and head back to the table. I can't believe Jesse's talking to the guests. What if Dad comes back?

That's when I notice the dishes aren't done.

Mom seems to be okay doing the puzzle, so I go to the sink.

Jesse comes out of the office waving a wad of cash, and I hear the guests' truck starting up. "He's renting Cabin Two for the night, with a boat, plus the gear," Jesse says, putting the cash under the ashtray on the end table next to Dad's recliner.

As I turn back to the sink, there's a big crashing noise behind me. Mom's on her feet and her chair's toppled over. "I thought you were going to help me with this puzzle!" she yells, sweeping her arm across the table. Jesse leaps forward, but he's too late. The puzzle box bounces off the wall, and pieces fly everywhere.

"I'm sorry, Mom," he says.

"Mom?" She looks around the room. "Where's Mom?"

I look at the clock. It says nine-fifteen. "Anna," I say, "it's past your bedtime."

She turns to look at the clock, too. "Holy cow," she says. "I'd better be in bed before Mom gets home." She shuffles into her room and closes the door.

Jesse picks up the chair and I turn back to the

dishes. That's when we hear the truck. I work as fast as I can, but it's too late. Dad's through the door with his arms full of groceries. He gets as far as the fridge, sets the bags down on the floor, sees a couple of puzzle pieces lying there, and freezes. Then his head jerks around and he sees the dishes aren't all dried and put away. He glares at me. "What the hell's been going on here?"

Jesse stands up, his hands full of puzzle pieces. "A guest came," he says, backing toward the door. I think about edging around so I can run, too, but Dad's too close, he'll just grab me. Jesse's using his careful voice. "I was busy renting out a cabin—"

Dad starts for him. Jesse drops the puzzle pieces and makes a run for it. I let out my breath and hurry to put away the last of the dishes. Macy rushes in with more groceries. She tries not to step on the puzzle pieces.

"Did Jesse get away?" I ask.

"Get the broom," she says. "Hurry. He was headed for the compound, but I don't know if he got enough of a head start." I use the broom to scoop puzzle pieces into the dustpan, dump them in the box, and stash everything properly in the closet. Macy's still rushing to put the groceries away, and I help her. Twelve loaves of bread and five big jugs of milk (most of it goes in the freezer). Lots of canned soup and stew. Oats, coffee, powdered juice, peanut butter...

"Good," I say. "You got marmalade."

"But only one jar," says Macy, hauling in another box of bread. Sniffing, she takes of her cap and hangs it on the peg. Her eyes are red. "Hurry, Drew."

I'm putting the last loaf in the freezer when the door busts open and Dad storms in. He stomps over to his recliner and grabs the cash from under the ashtray. He starts counting it. Macy and I look at each other, then back at Dad, watching him.

"Two twenty-five," Dad says, stuffing the cash into his wallet. "Karma. Mom sleeping?"

I nod.

"You kids get out there and get at the raking. I got paperwork to do."

Macy and I grab our caps and hurry up the road toward the compound. It's still chilly because the trees are tall here and the sun hasn't had a chance to warm up the road. When we get to the compound, the big front gate is unlocked. I help Macy push it open a bit so we can squeeze through, and then we close it behind us. The chain link makes a tinkling sound as the gate moves. The metal's cold on my hands.

The shed door's open and Jesse's coming out with a jerry can. He grins at us, goes around the shed to the gas tank, twists the lock open and starts filling the can.

"I thought he'd catch you," Macy says.

"Nah. I was already over the gate," says Jesse. "Time he got it open, I was over the back gate, too. How was your little outing?"

Macy clamps her lips shut.

Jesse laughs, locking the pump. "Figured he'd be mad about having to buy groceries," he says. "Good thing we were out of stuff he eats, too. Hey, Macy, the Forresters loaned me a bike this morning. Wanna go riding with us tomorrow?"

Macy looks at him. Her eyes get big. "Jesse, have you lost your mind?"

"Don't you remember what it felt like to ride a bike? It's like flying." He screws the spout back onto the jerry can and pulls the gate open enough to squeeze through. "Let me know if you change your mind."

Macy watches him slide the gate closed. Then she comes over to the back of the shed and helps me pull the rakes and the shovel out of the tool barrel.

There's other tools in the barrel that can make it fall over if you're not careful. One of them is a scythe. It looks like the one carried by the scary guy in the fairytale book Mom used to read to us. She said he was called Death, or the Grim Reaper. And Jesse told me Death uses his scythe to kill people.

Macy holds the other tools while I pull out the tools we need, because I don't like to touch the scythe. It makes me feel kind of scared just to look at it. One day Dad was carrying it, and I thought maybe he was going to kill somebody with it, just like the Grim Reaper. But instead he just used it to cut the long grass behind Cabin Four where the mower can't go.

That was because one of the guests said the grass was a fire hazard, and Dad better deal with it before someone reported it. Dad says the last thing he needs is some nosy bureaucrat sniffing around.

He didn't say anything like that to the guest, though. He just said, "Thank you for sharing your concern," which is what he likes to say to people's faces. While he was getting the scythe, he said some other words. But he sliced down the long grass and Jesse and me loaded it into the wheelbarrow and hauled it up to the compost. Cutting the grass riled up the mosquitoes so much the guest couldn't stay on his porch and watch, because he was getting bit. Once he'd gone inside, Dad laughed and said that karma was a real bitch.

That reminds me. "Macy, why is two hundred and twenty-five dollars a karma?"

We're raking the playground and no one's around, so it's okay to talk, but Macy still looks toward the lodge.

"You mean what Dad said about the money?"

I nod.

"The groceries cost two twenty-three," she says, raking pinecones and needles and small branches into a pile.

"Oh." I scoop a load of pinecones and dump them into the wheelbarrow. "That's not really what a karma is, though. Is it?"

She shakes her head. "I don't think so," she says. "But it's a good thing Jesse got him that money, because otherwise Dad would have been short when Mr. Blade comes tomorrow."

Short. Oh.

I guess that's why Dad was in such a bad mood. Last time Dad was short, we were at Mosquito Lake. Mr. Blade said the boss wasn't going to be happy. So Dad got Mom to give Mr. Blade some of her jewellery, too. But the boss still wasn't happy. The next time Mr. Blade was supposed to come, it wasn't Mr. Blade. It was some other guy. Dad had extra money by then because he sold our car, so the other guy just made his knuckles crack at Dad and said it was a damn good thing he'd learned his lesson.

Jesse said he thought the other guy's name was Bagman, but I'm pretty sure I heard Mom tell Dad that Mr. Blade wasn't his friend, just another bagman. So maybe that's not a name, but a job, like a farmer or a teacher. I tried looking it up in the dictionary but it went from baggataway, which is a game of the First Nations of eastern Canada from which lacrosse was developed, straight to bagpipes. I already knew what those are, because once we got stuck in traffic because of a parade and some guys wearing skirts and weird hats were making noise with bagpipes.

I tried looking under the word bag, too, but they only had bag lady, which means a homeless woman carrying all her possessions in shopping bags. Maybe that guy left all his shopping bags in the car. But I don't think so.

Mr. Bagman had come to see Dad once before, back when we lived in Kelowna. I liked that house. It was closer to Grandma's and Jesse and Macy could ride their bikes and I could walk to kindergarten and grade one. But right after Mr. Bagman came we moved to Platt's Landing and we never saw Grandma again.

Also Mom home schooled us, which I liked because I didn't have to keep waiting for the other kids to catch up.

Jesse liked Platt's Landing better than Mosquito Lake because when he wasn't doing chores, he could go play in the bush. We didn't have a TV to watch because Dad said it rots kids' brains and gives them the notion they can backtalk their elders, and we'd already picked up too much of that crap at school.

Jesse said he didn't miss school but he wanted to move back to Kelowna where there were kids to play with. But Mom said we'd lost the house. I thought that was funny. I asked her how a house can get lost. She said it was still there, but we had to sell it. And then she started to cry so I stopped asking questions.

I want to ask Macy if she'd rather go back to Kelowna, or to Mosquito Lake, or to Platt's Landing, but we're raking by the cabins now so we don't talk.

I liked Platt's Landing okay. We had a big chicken barn there. It was all full of chickens, and it was my job to help collect the eggs. Dad took the eggs to town to sell them for money, but once I heard him telling Mr. Blade that eggs aren't much of a cash crop compared to weeds, and a lot more trouble.

Weeds sure are easy to grow, so I wonder why people pay for them. I guess it's like when they buy worms for fishing. They don't like to get their hands dirty.

You need to know where to look to find worms. They like it under boards and rocks, and they really like the compost pile. That's where Jesse and Macy and I put the weeds that grow here at Keneece, after we take them out of the flower beds. They keep growing back, though.

There are lots of different kinds of weeds, like dandelions and crabgrass and those ones that grow little pea pods. That one's my favourite. When we lived at Platt's Landing we didn't have to help Dad with the weeds. Maybe because we didn't have flower beds, or because it was winter and we did school with Mom.

Dad didn't have to dig the weeds out of the snow, though. They were growing under the big chicken barn in something called a bunker. Mr. Blade said some crazy survivalists had built it years ago.

There are three kinds of bunker in the dictionary. One's a sandy hollow on a golf course. Another's a place to store fuel on a ship. The third kind of bunker is a steel-and-concrete fortification built partly or wholly underground. That must be the kind of bunker that was under the barn.

I think the boss might have owned the farm at

Platt's Landing, because Mr. Blade said Dad owed the boss too much money and getting the crop off was the only way he could work it off and keep all his fingers.

Mr. Blade must have been right, because Dad's fingers are still all there.

Mom cried a lot at Platt's Landing, but only when Dad wasn't looking. I think she missed Grandma. We didn't have a telephone there, so Mom couldn't even call her. She wrote Grandma a couple of letters but she never heard back. Two times when we went to the mailbox in Vernon so Dad could pick up the mail I thought there was a letter from Grandma in it, but both times he said it was nothing but a damn bill and tore it up and threw it in the garbage with the rest of them, right there at the mailbox.

Dad said Grandma didn't want to talk to us ever again, and maybe he was right.

Jesse didn't like it when Grandma visited, because it always made Dad be in a bad mood. After Grandma went home, he'd make Mom cry. He didn't always hit her, just sometimes. So Jesse said if Grandma really loved us, she would just stay away.

But I think maybe missing Grandma was what started Mom feeling sadder and sadder. And then when the boss said we were finished and someone else had to work a crop, Mom thought we could maybe move back to Kelowna.

Dad didn't want to go back there, and when Mr. Blade told him about a summer job at

Mosquito Lake, he figured that would be perfect.

Mom seemed to like it okay there, but she was still sad.

Once when we went to Vernon to get money from the ATM, and we still had Grace so she had to stay in the car for insurance instead of me, Mom tried to use a payphone to call Grandma but it didn't work. And Mosquito Lake Lodge had a phone so Mom tried to call Grandma a couple of times when Dad was out, but the number still didn't work right because it was somebody else's answering machine.

When Dad saw the phone bill he told Mom she must not like her kids much, taking chances like that, so she didn't try any more. And then when Dad gave Grace away to some people who wanted her, he and Mom had a real big fight, and he held her by the chin and whacked her head up into the wall. The next day she was really sick, and Dad said she must've had a stroke, and after that Mom was just too sad to ever be herself again.

Macy's wheeling the wheelbarrow back up to the compound. She's twelve now, and almost as tall as Mom. I'm still too small to wheel the wheelbarrow, so I'm carrying the tools. Once we're past Cabin Four it's okay to talk again, so I ask, "If you could fly, where would you go?"

She sighs and sets the wheelbarrow down, and I help her open the gate wide enough to wheel it through. That's when I see she's still crying.

"Drew," she says, wiping her arm across her eyes, "I don't want to talk about it."

In the corner of the compound a couple of birds are fighting over a piece of garbage, and Macy makes a face at them. I'm glad there are only a few today. Sometimes there's a bunch of them squawking and fighting, and once in a while something makes them all come flapping out of the pit. Macy says they creep her out.

I help her dump the wheelbarrow into the compost and she holds the tools back while I put the rakes and the shovel away and pull out the pitchfork. She uses it to mix the needles into the dirt, then hands it back to me so I can put it back into the barrel.

The sun's higher now. I look up and see it gleaming off the blade of the scythe.

Thursday, July 26

I finish sweeping the paths and the porch before the rain starts, but I'm not allowed to go inside because Mr. Blade is in there. Mom was already having her nap, so he went back out to his car and got a case of beer and then went in to talk to Dad for a while.

The wind tugs at my cap and I pull it down tighter on my head. The storm's blowing pine-cones out of the trees, so Macy and I will probably need to rake again after she's done cleaning the cabins. A few more pine needles fall onto the porch and I sweep them off the edge.

There's a line of ants scurrying down the wall from the office window. They're going along the porch and around the corner of the lodge. Then they go along the wall, just above the ground, until they get to a place under the big window that's by the kitchen table. That's where Dad and Mr. Blade are having their beers. I can hear the bumble-dee bumble of them talking. I crouch down so they won't see me.

The ants go down onto the ground here under the window. Then they climb up a little mound of dirt and disappear into the top of a tiny volcano. It's not really a volcano. There's no lava or steam or ash. It's just shaped like one. Other ants are coming out of the volcano, going back along the same trail. They don't bump into each other, though. They are making two lines, one for going out, the other for coming back. The ones that are coming back are carrying some white stuff. Maybe it's sugar.

Behind me, in the house, someone's walking toward the window. I stay close to the wall. It must be Mr. Blade because now I can hear his voice through the window, even though it's closed. He's talking about the weather. Grownups do that a lot. "Damn storm's getting worse," he says. "Lookit the waves on that lake. Say, didja hear about the body they found in Wood Lake last week? Cops were all over it, all proud they'd found another of the Kingpin Crew." He snorts. "A hit like that, cops find a body, they gotta know it's cuz the pros want it found. Nothing to do with them. Hey, Jack, you know the best way to get rid of a body, don't you?"

My dad says something. It sounds like bumble-dee bumble.

"Nah, you never bury it," says Mr. Blade. "Amateur mistake. Ya just strip it and dump it in the bush, scavengers'll do the rest. Burn the clothes and there's nothin' ta bumble-dee bumble..." His footsteps fade back toward the table.

Even more ants are coming out of the little volcano, hundreds of them. They must really like

that sugar. I wonder how far down into the
ground they take it. Maybe they just drop the
tiny bit they're carrying and it falls right onto a
giant sugar pile. Or maybe it slides down a long
tunnel and then drops onto the big pile. Or maybe
once the ants are in the ground they walk a long
ways through a series of tunnels, hauling it to a
secret chamber deep in the ground. Or the secret
chamber could be under our house. Maybe right
under the kitchen. Or my bedroom. Or both.
Wouldn't it be cool if they had a whole ant palace
down there, with huge caverns full of sugar and
maybe some jam and other stuff, too.

Thunder rumbles and echoes over the lake.
Macy comes out of Cabin Two, pushes her cap
back and looks up at the sky. Then she squeezes
the water out of her mop and goes back in. Jesse's
just coming up from the boathouse with the
green tub, and I get out from under the window,
straighten up my legs, and follow him back up to
the porch. Jesse sees Mr. Blade's car. "Hey,
who's here?" he asks.

"Mr. Blade has a new car," I say.

"Another one?" Jesse whistles. He takes a bag
of garbage from his tub and tosses it into the
back of the lodge truck to make it look like he's
working, but he's actually taking a good look at
Mr. Blade's car. This one is big and black. It kind
of reminds me of the one Grandma used to come
in, back when we lived in Kelowna. Sometimes
her driver would stay in the car waiting for her,
reading a newspaper or a book. But he always

got out and opened the door for her and helped her get in. He always helped her get out of the car, too. He called Grandma "ma'am," and if it was slippery he would let her hold his arm and he'd walk all the way to the front door with her. But he never went inside the house for coffee.

Once when he came back to the car he saw me at the front of it. I was looking at the letter B with wings. It should have been a C, for car. I might have said that out loud, instead of just thinking it, because he said "B is for Best. Or for Bentley." And he winked at me.

Jesse's tub has got more than life jackets and fishing tackle in it. There's some cans of beer and a bottle with a picture of a turkey. "Those people left these in the boat," he says. "Dad'll probably want them." He sets the tub under the porch and pulls out a couple of pails, hands one to me, and we crouch down to start weeding the flowerbeds on either side of the front walkway. I've pulled three dandelions and a couple of clumps of crabgrass when Macy comes up from the cabins with her buckets full of rags and glass cleaner and her mop. Suddenly she stands still and her eyes get big.

Jesse looks over his shoulder to see what she's staring at. He looks back at her and shakes his head. "It's Mr. Blade's new car," he says.

Macy kind of shrinks. She looks like she's going to start crying again.

Jesse glances toward the front door. "Better get moving," he says.

Macy puts her mop and buckets under the porch. She rubs the back of her hand across her eyes and crouches down alongside Jesse.

"She's not coming," says Jesse.

"She will," says Macy, kind of fierce, yanking out a handful of crabgrass and throwing it into his pail. "She loves us."

They're talking about Grandma. Macy's still waiting for her to show up like she used to. But once Jesse told her that if Grandma really loves us, she'll leave us alone, because every time Grandma comes for a visit Dad starts to boil. That sounds stupid, but I know what he means. It's when Dad gets kind of red all over and he looks like he's going to explode. He'd get red when Grandma was around, and then after she left, he would bust out yelling and hitting and stuff like that. Just like a pot that's boiling over.

But when Jesse told Macy that Grandma should leave us alone, Macy got really mad at him. I don't mean they had a fight. I saw some kids at school having a real fight once. They were punching each other, and they sure got into trouble for that. Macy and Jesse don't ever even yell at each other.

Except that one time, Macy looked like maybe she wanted to punch Jesse. Oh, I just remembered. One time Jesse did call Macy a bad name. Grandma heard him and boy, she wasn't happy about it. She told Mom that our young Jesse was sounding a bit too much like Jack for her liking.

Mom didn't like that. Jesse didn't either. He

said he'd never, ever grow up to be anything like Dad. And then Mom cried.

So maybe that's another reason why Jesse doesn't want Grandma to come.

Right now Macy's pretending she isn't crying, but she is. Except she doesn't look sad. She looks mad.

They're almost done their side of the path, and Jesse sits back on his heels. "Macy," he says, and he's using his calm voice, the one he uses when Mom's upset, "if Grandma could come, she would."

I wonder, why can't she come? Grandma is pretty old. She's Mom's grandma too. Mom's parents would have been my grandparents, except they died in a car accident when Mom was a kid. And so did Mom's brother, Arty. He would have been my uncle. That's when Grandma came back home from Europe to look after Mom. And she was already old.

Now she's really old, so she can't drive any more. But she could get her driver to bring her to see us. Or, if she was sick, she could send her driver to say hi to Mom. That happened a couple of times in Kelowna. And even if her car has got broken down like ours did, she could just go get another one because she has lots of money. Dad says she's loaded.

That didn't sound right to me because when Dad gets loaded it's because he's been drinking lots of beer, but Grandma doesn't drink. So I checked in the dictionary. There's more than one kind of loaded. When Dad's loaded it means the same as drunk. But loaded also means rich. That's the kind of loaded that Grandma is.

And Jesse says that's why Dad married Mom.

The thunder rumbles again, and a couple of pinecones plop onto the roof and then roll down. They bounce off the porch, so I keep weeding.

Macy's not weeding. She's staring at Jesse. "What do you mean, she can't come? She isn't... did she die?"

"I don't think so," Jesse says quickly. He's still using his extra-kind voice. "She just doesn't know where we are." He comes over to my side of the path and crouches down to help.

I'm pretty sure he's right about Grandma. She can't be dead, because when that happens Mom will get lots of money all at one time, instead of just her measly allowance on the tenth and the twenty-fifth of each month. Dad says two grand a month is chicken scratch, and he can't wait for the old lady to croak. Which I looked up, and it means the same as die.

Macy pulls up a few more weeds, picks up the pail and comes around to join us. "But Grandma didn't come see us at Platt's Landing, either. Mom wrote to her so she must have known where we were."

Jesse shakes his head. "Dad mailed all the letters," he says. "He always read them first. Once Mom must have sort of hinted where we were, because Dad made her write a different letter instead. Same thing last summer when we were at Mosquito Lake Resort. So even if Grandma did figure out we were at Platt's Landing, she wouldn't know where we went after that. And Mom can't write letters since she had the stroke, so there's no way Grandma knows where we are now."

"But Grandma said she wouldn't let any money go into Mom's account if she doesn't hear from her," says Macy.

"I know," says Jesse. "But remember last winter, just after we moved here to Keneece, when Dad was all happy because he found out the money's in a trust?"

"What does that mean?" Macy asks.

"I don't know," Jesse says, and they both look at me.

I try to think if I've ever read about what a trust is. "I'll check the dictionary," I say.

"Anyway," says Jesse, "Dad said Grandma couldn't hold that over him any more." Dad also said the old bat only ever cared about the money, but I hope Jesse won't tell Macy that. Besides, I think Grandma did love us, too. Mom always told her to use some of her money to go travel and enjoy life, but Grandma said she just wanted to see her great-grandchildren grow up.

But maybe after she couldn't find us, she gave up and went back to Europe.

Macy frowns. "Grandma could still find us. When Mom wrote to her from Platt's Landing, our address was on the envelope."

Jesse shakes his head. "That's the number for

the box at the post office in Vernon," he says. "It didn't say where we lived. We were out in the middle of nowhere."

Macy's starting to cry again.

"She could hire a detective," I say. "Or she could get the police."

Jesse looks at me. "Remember the last time the police came?"

I don't, really. But I know that after they came, Dad was gone for a while, to stay with some people called Deetocks at their farm. And I remember what happened then. Everybody was happy. Mom, too. And then Dad came back, and he was nicer, just like Mom said he would be. That's when she said we were finally a real family. And we still had Baby Grace and our Kelowna house and everything.

But only for a couple of days. And then Grandma said Dad was starting to act like the old Jack again. Grandma said Dad can charm the birds out of the trees when he wants to, which was how Mom got into this mess in the first place. She said Dad had pulled the wool over the judge's eyes too, which was how he got sent to the Deetocks instead of jail. And then Dad told Mom that if her busybody old bitch of a grandmother ever sicked the cops on him again, we'd all be sorry.

Macy's still trying hard to stop crying. I want to tell her about our plan to go and get Grace, but Jesse still didn't say it was okay to tell, so I don't. Sometimes we all need to keep secrets

from each other. That makes it easier to stop
Dad from finding out.

I pick up the weed pails and watch the dust
blowing out from behind Mr. Blade's car. It goes
swirling in the wind and up into the trees.

Macy's gathering her cleaning supplies and
Jesse's pulling the tub out from under the porch.
Then I see Dad's on the top step, glaring at me.
"Takes three of you to weed one puny flower-
bed?" he says, and I get ready to drop my stuff
and scatter so he can't catch all three of us at
once. But then he sees what Jesse has in the tub.

"Well, what've we got here? Rye and a six
pack chaser," he says, grabbing the turkey bottle.
"Get that beer into the fridge. And wash your
damn hands." He goes back in the house, letting
the screen door slam behind him. Macy climbs
the stairs, sets one of her buckets down and
opens the screen for Jesse. I set the weed pails in
the back of the truck. The garbage Dad and Jesse
collected from the cabins this morning is still in
there. The birds will find it soon.

I sweep a few more pine needles off the porch.
There's laughing and shouting down by Cabin
One. That's the Forresters. Their boat is back at
their dock, and they're hurrying to unload it. I
check on the ants. They are still travelling back
and forth, too. It's like everyone's trying to finish
their chores before the storm gets worse.

Jesse comes back out with the truck keys. He

sets the blocks on the pedals and puts the cushion on the driver's seat and climbs in. The starter makes a noise but the truck doesn't start. He cranks her over a couple of times the way Dad told him to, and the engine catches.

The thunder rumbles again, even louder than the lodge truck. Jesse rolls the window down. "Hey Drew, can you come give me a hand with unloading?"

I run around to the passenger side and climb in, and we head for the compound. Jesse unhooks the gate key from the rest of them and leaves the truck running while we slide the gate open. He drives through, goes close to the shed, then swings around and stops beside the pit.

Dad dug this pit with the lodge tractor. It's in the corner of the compound where we got the boats and picnic tables from, in the spring, after the snow was gone. In the winter it was easy to get rid of the garbage. We burnt up lots of it in the wood stove in the lodge. Not the plastic stuff because that was too stinky. We burnt that up in the burning barrel in the compound. But when the guests came Dad said some idiot would report us for burning trash, so we had to separate the tin cans and squish them and take all the trash to the transfer station.

Those are all pretty far away. There's one in Cherryville, kind of on the way to Mosquito Lake. We had to use that one a couple of times when we lived up there, because there were ATVs for rent at Mosquito Lake and you never know when one of the ATVers is going to turn out to be one of those damn environmentalists and go squealing to the bureaucrats.

The Lumby one's on Trinity Valley Road, which is funny because that's also the road to Platt's Landing. But when we lived there we never went to the transfer station. We burned all our garbage in a barrel out back.

And there's another really big dump place in Vernon that we went to once. It's all the way up on top of a hill.

When we lived at Mosquito Lake we went to all those places. That's because Dad says it's best to distribute your stuff in case Grandma's spies are looking for our DNA. Also, he says patterns are a good way to get busted. That's how come he never took Mom to the same ATM twice in a row.

Anyway, Dad says if the bureaucrats really want him to use the appropriate facilities, they'd put them somewhere more convenient. Besides, it's also a stupid damn waste of time and fuel to haul garbage to the transfer station at Cherryville when there is perfectly good unused real estate available right here.

So that's why he dug the pit. It's a secret from the Cornells, though. He put the gravel he dug out of the pit into a big pile. He says when the season's over he's going to put it back on top of the garbage and then put the boats and tables on top of that, and no one will be the wiser.

It's starting to rain now, and there's not as

many seconds between the thunder rumble and the lightning. The birds are rising up out of the garbage pit and circling over us, screaming. They probably want to be fed. The exhaust from the truck stinks. It's also making a steam cloud. I reach over the tailgate to get the weed pails.

Jesse's gone to the tool barrel to get the pitch-fork. The barrel wobbles and I hold my breath, but it doesn't fall over. I bring the buckets over and dump them onto the compost. Jesse's finished throwing the garbage into the pit, and the birds are settling in for a feast.

"Heads up." Jesse tosses the pitchfork over near me. I pick it up and start churning the weeds into the compost. When I'm done, Jesse's already driving the truck back through the gate. I turn the pitchfork upside down, making sure I'm not going to hit the scythe, and carefully slide its handle down into the tool barrel.

Then I run through the pouring rain to help him close the gate.

We're soaked. Thunder crashes again. Jesse hikes himself up onto the cushion and fumbles to get the gate key back onto the key ring, then pulls off his cap and shakes off the water, laughing. "Great storm," he says, "real gully-washer." That's something Grandma used to say.

I think Jesse actually does like Grandma.

Jesse pulls his cap back on. Then he digs into his pocket. "Look here," he says. He opens his hand. At first I think it's an orange fishing lure, but it isn't.

"It's a Swiss army knife," he says.

It doesn't look like a knife to me. "Where's the blade?" I ask.

"Right here, see?" He turns it sideways and shows me. The sides of the knife are silver, with little grooves. Jesse puts his thumbnail into one of the grooves and pulls, and a blade glides out.

"What are those other grooves?" I ask.

"Bottle opener, scissors, another blade..." He shows me. "And look at this twisty thing, here."

"What's it for"

"Dunno," he says. "But it's pretty cool, huh? It was left in the boat with the beer."

Jesse puts the blades and the scissors and the twisty thing back into the handle of the knife, and pushes it deep into his pocket.

"Is this a secret?"

He grins, shifts the truck into gear, and we head back to the lodge.

Monday, August 6

Mom's just about done her puzzle for the third time. Today's Monday, so it's the one with the horses, a mother horse and a colt. Macy's done putting the dishes away. She looks at the clock, and then goes to look out the windows again. She's looking for Jesse.

In the morning Jesse usually does outside chores with Dad. They get garbage from the cabins and clean up the boats. Sometimes the boats have to be bailed, but it hasn't rained for a while, not since the day Mr. Blade was here, and that was almost two weeks ago now.

Today is different, though. Jesse must be outside doing the chores by himself, because Dad is still here. And he's still sleeping. When I went to bed last night he was still out visiting with the guests. I wonder if Jesse was, too. Probably not.

A car comes up from down at the lake and parks outside, and there's footsteps on the porch. A key rattles in the drop box and the footsteps go back down the steps. Macy peeks out the window in the front door.

"There goes Cabin Four," she says. Her mop

and cleaning stuff is already by the door, along with the laundry basket. She puts on her cap. "I'll bring you up the sheets so you can get the laundry started."

Usually Monday is a good day to do our own laundry, but today Monday's part of a long weekend. That means it's more like a Sunday, which is a checkout day, so there's guest laundry to do instead. I start the washing. If it isn't raining, once Mom's back in bed I can hang the pillowcases and towels and dishcloths out back on the clothesline. But I have to wait for Macy or Jesse to help me hang up the sheets. If it is raining, I'll just use the stool and put them in the dryer instead.

Mom's singing a song about a woman named Sweet Caroline. She hums the parts where she forgets the words. "Mmm, mmm, mmm, Sweet Caroline, buh, buh, buh, something something something good. I something something buh, buh, buh, to la something lala la la la and la la. Mm mm mmm mmmm..."

She doesn't know me today.

Macy's been gone a few minutes when Mom stops singing. She stops working on the puzzle, too. Then she starts to rock back and forth in her chair. Usually this means she's going to get mad and throw stuff. Sometimes it means she's going to start to cry. Right now I can't tell if she's mad or sad.

"Hey, Anna," I say. "Nice job on this puzzle."

She stops rocking. "Puzzle?' she says.

"Puzzle," I say. "I like the horses."

"I don't," she says. "I hate horses." She looks like she might be getting mad.

"Even the cute baby ones?" I say, running my finger over the colt.

She looks down at the horses, and her eyes go squinty. Just then Macy comes back.

"Who's this?" Mom asks.

Macy hands me the laundry basket. "Just me. Macy, the laundry lady," she says.

"Oh. Hello," says Mom. She picks up the last puzzle piece and fits it into place. "Look what I made! Cute horses."

"Very nice," says Macy. She looks at me and raises her eyebrows. "Jesse?"

I shake my head, put some soap in with the sheets, and start the machine.

Macy looks like she wants to say something, but then she just bites on her bottom lip and heads back out.

Mom crumples up the puzzle, then she starts turning all the pieces right side up. "Sweet Caroline," she sings, "buh, buh, buh..."

I wonder if that woman is called sweet Caroline because she likes sugar. After I finish the laundry, I might go see how the ants are doing. A couple of days after that big storm I noticed they weren't coming to the office any more, so I put some sugar on the ground out by the porch. I thought about putting it right in their volcano, but I like watching them carry it.

I might dig into the volcano a little ways to

see where they're taking it. I haven't decided yet.

"Nine-fifteen," says Mom. "Time for bed." She goes to the bathroom to pee and brush her teeth, and I start cleaning up the puzzle. When she comes out of the bathroom, she stops in the doorway and looks at me. "Where's my hug?" she asks.

I set down the puzzle. She shuffles a couple steps forward with her arms open, and I try to turn my nose off. Mom used to give really good hugs, but now she has a funny smell. She's really boney, too, not soft like she used to be. And also her belly kind of sticks out in the way, too. But she wraps me in her arms and just for a moment it's like she's my Mom again. "I love you," she says, kissing me on the top of my head.

I don't care how she smells. I just want her to hold onto me forever.

The phone rings, and Mom ignores it. She's still hugging me. But then the bedroom door flies open and Dad knocks us out of his way as he stomps to the office.

"G'night, Dad," Mom chirps. She pats my shoulder. "G'night, Arty." She shuffles off to bed.

I pick up the puzzle box, put it away in the closet, and fill the kettle for Dad's coffee.

Macy's done Cabin Four so she's helping me hang the sheets. Even though the stoop is pretty high up, we have to fold them in half, first, so they won't drag on the ground. Macy looks like she's been crying. And she keeps looking down the hill to the boat house.

"He's probably digging worms," I say, keeping my voice really quiet.

Macy pegs her end of the sheet to the line, and I pass her more of the sheet and another clothes peg.

"Dad saw him..." she chokes.

"What?" I ask.

Macy takes a deep breath. "Last night Dad came back before Jesse."

I pass her some more sheet and another peg. Her hands are shaking. "Was he loaded?" I ask.

Macy nods.

Somewhere up the lake, a loon calls out.

We bend down to fold another sheet, and Macy takes a deep breath. "I was getting Mom to bed when Dad saw him go by on the..." She swallows.

"With the Forresters?" I ask.

She nods.

I hand her a peg. "What happened?"

"Dad went out for a couple of minutes, and I thought he was going to the Forresters to get him," Macy says. Now she's talking really fast, like she can't stop herself. "Then he came back and waited. When Jesse opened the door and saw Dad waiting for him, he knew he was in for it. So he ran."

She finishes pegging up the sheet and picks up the laundry basket.

"He'll be okay," I say as we walk back around to the front door. "Jesse's fast, and he's smart."

Then we stop talking because we're almost at the porch, and Mr. Forrester is there to check out. "Hey, kids," he says.

Macy and I are saying "Hi, Mr. Forrester," but Dad's interrupting.

"There you are," he says. He's using his nice voice that he saves for in front of the guests. He twists the gate key off his key ring. "Quick like rabbits, kids, go and get me some worms. We have guests down at the boathouse waiting for some. Get a couple dozen down there, pronto."

Even when Dad uses his nice voice he still means business, so Macy and I hurry to the compound. Macy unlocks the gate and we slide it open. She gets a cleaned-out soup can from the shed and then holds the tools while I pull out the pitchfork. For once, there aren't a bunch of screaming birds in the pit. We can hear them out back on the other side of the compound, up the road to where the old dump was, up past the tall tree. I'm glad for Macy, because she already looks like Mom used to when she said one of us was on her last nerve. The last thing Macy will want to deal with is those creepy birds.

I scoop some dirt into the soup can, and we dig and dig in the compost and finally come up with twenty-four worms. A couple of them are a bit small, but Dad did tell us to hurry. We put the pitchfork away, squeeze through the gate and close it, and hurry down to the boathouse.

Whoever wanted the worms must've got tired of waiting.

I wonder if we're in for it now. We head back up the hill to the lodge. The Forresters' car is heading up the driveway. Up on their roof rack, some of the bicycles' wheels are spinning as if someone is riding them. But nobody is. And the bikes are upside down.

Dad's sitting on the porch. Macy hands him the gate key. "Well, it's about time," he says, standing up and heading for the truck. "Might as well take those worms back where you got them from. Guests didn't want to wait. Macy, you best get down to Cabin One and get it mucked out. And you two are both going to have to start pulling your weight around here," he says, climbing into the truck. "Your brother's decided he'd rather live with the Forresters. He just packed up his stuff and left."

The truck starts up on the first try.

Dad slams the door, puts it in gear, and heads toward the compound.

Macy turns and runs into the lodge. When I get to our bedroom, she's down on her knees looking under the bunk. She slowly gets to her feet, and looks up at Jesse's bunk. The sheets and everything are all lying in a pile on the bare mattress, but under the bunk Jesse's backpack is gone. She closes her eyes, turns and flings herself down on her own bed, sobbing.

Friday, August 10

"C'mon, Drew." It's still dark when Macy shakes me awake. "Drew, please, I have to go."

I make myself sit up. Macy's got something in her hands. It's Mom's scarf and glasses.

"Just let the fire go out," she whispers. "I stoked it up, so it should keep going long enough. If Mom's too cold, turn on the electric oven and open the door. Just be sure to get it turned off before eight so it's cooled before we get back."

I nod.

"Mom should sleep for a few more minutes," she says. "We'll be..."

There's footsteps outside the bedroom door, and in the light from the kitchen I can see Dad standing there. He clears his throat.

"Coming," Macy says.

I get out of bed and open the curtains. I can barely make out the nest in the big tree. Looks like it's still empty. I leave the bedroom door open so I can see to put on my clothes. Then I straighten out my bed, but I'm not sure I've done a good job. There's a light switch in our room, but we're not supposed to use it. Jesse had it on once to finish reading a comic book he'd found in the boathouse and Dad took the bulb away. Lucky Dad didn't see it was a comic book or Jesse'd have got a whupping. Jesse said he'd been reading one of the National Geographic magazines the Cornells had left behind, and that's when Dad took the whole pile out from under the bunk. Next day he hauled them all up to the burning barrel.

I wonder if the Cornells will be mad about that.

The Cornells are the people who own Keneece Lake Resort, but Mrs. Cornell is real sick so last September Mr. Cornell took her to Mexico to try to make her better. Dad said it was a lucky break for us, because the Thompsons weren't about to let us spend the winter up at Mosquito Lake Lodge. Dad phoned Mr. Thompson a couple of times to try to get him to change his mind, but Mr. Thompson said no way he could afford it.

Then at the end of last summer Mr. Thompson called to say the Cornells were going away and Keneece Lake Resort gets vandalized in the winter by yahoos so the Cornells needed a caretaker until spring, to keep the yahoos away. Dad used the Thompsons' camp truck to move us down here. He took a bunch of their groceries, too. He said the Thompsons had paid him diddly squat to have him work his fingers to the bone all summer, and that Mom had worked so hard for them she'd even had a stroke, too, so the Thompsons owed us. And besides, what they didn't know wouldn't hurt them.

He did take the truck back up to their place, though. And Mr. Blade gave him a ride back down to Keneece. Mr. Blade was at Mosquito Lake to collect some plants he had growing up there in the bush.

Mr. Blade said Mosquito Lake was a sweet set-up, but Keneece had even better growing conditions.

In spring, Mr. Cornell phoned Dad and said Mrs. Cornell was getting sicker instead of better. Dad told him that he and Mom could run Keneece for the summer, no problem.

And the next time Mr. Blade came, he had a good look around. He went exploring up the road that used to go out to the old dump, on the other side of the compound, but he said the bush there was too steep and rocky to be any damn good. Dad showed him out the other side of the lodge, past Cabin One, where there's a walking path that goes along the lake for a while and then up to the road. Mr. Blade said that was too damn public. But the next time he came he borrowed a boat and went exploring and when he got back he said there was a nice little meadow up the lake, with good arable land.

I'd read about arable land in a National Geographic. It means it's good for a farm. So maybe Mr. Blade is a farmer.

National Geographic had some good stories in it, and lots of really good pictures to show what they were talking about. I wish I still had them. Jesse felt really bad about it when Dad burnt them all. After that a guest left a stack of Reader's Digests in a boat. Jesse found a hiding place for them up in the compound, up in the back of the shed. I don't get much chance to read them, though.

I still don't think my bed's made right. I'll have to remember to come back when it's lighter out. I get to the kitchen before Mom wakes up. I hope she didn't wake up with an accident. Taking care of that is Macy's chore, but Jesse used to do it when Macy had to go to town to get the money. I can do the sheets, but I never had to help Mom get a bath.

I fill the kettle with water and plug it in. Mostly Mom doesn't ever want coffee any more, but sometimes she does. She'd probably like some hot chocolate. Maybe I should see if Macy can get some next time they buy groceries. Once, some guests left some hot chocolate mix in one of the cabins and Macy brought it up to the lodge. Jesse said we should have just one cup a week to make it last. The next week we were going to have some but Dad had already drank the rest.

It's been four days now since Jesse went to live with the Forresters. Macy was really sad at first, but then after a while she got kind of mad instead. I haven't asked her why. We don't get to talk much because I'm always supposed to be helping Dad with the chores that Jesse used to do. I try to stay awake at night until Macy comes to bed, but by the time she gets Mom settled I'm always asleep.

One morning I woke up before Macy, so I waited until she was awake and then I tried to talk to her. That's when I found out she was mad. I asked her if she thought Jesse might come back but she just said she didn't care. He's gone off and left us behind and she doesn't want to talk about him ever again.

The kettle whistles, and I'm just getting out the toaster when Mom comes running out of her room. "Oh, oh, oh," she says, tugging at her pajamas. She forgets to close the bathroom door and I hear the toilet lid clank open. "Oh, oh, oh," she says again, and then I can hear her peeing. "Whew," she says. "Made it."

I plug in the toaster, drop in a couple of slices of bread, and push down the lever. Mom's washing her hands. "My, what a rat's nest," she says, and I hear the bathroom drawer open. When she comes into the kitchen, she's tugging the brush through her hair. "Good morning, Drew. You're up early. It's barely light out."

I stop moving. "Hi Mom," I say.

She smiles at me. "Where is everyone?" She's heading to her bedroom.

I want to follow her, but the toast pops. "They went to town," I say.

I pull out the toast and put in a couple more

slices of bread. When I turn around, Mom's in the doorway to her bedroom. The hairbrush is kind of stuck in her hair. She's holding it and just standing still, staring into her room.

"Mom?" I say.

Mom slowly pulls the hairbrush out of her hair and turns to look at me. "What is this place?" she asks.

"We're at Keneece Lake Lodge," I tell her. "That's your room."

"Are we on vacation?" she asks, looking at the table, the cupboards, the front door.

"Yes," I say. "Breakfast's ready."

"Oh," she says, but she's still just standing there. Then she looks down. Her eyes get big. "Oh, no," she says. She drops the brush and puts both hands on her belly. "Oh, no, no, no." She looks up at me. "Drew, where is Grace?"

I try to say something, but I can't think of anything. Mom moves toward our bedroom door. "Grace?" she calls. I make my legs move so I can follow her. She's reaching in for the light switch, flicking it up and down but there's no bulb. "Grace!"

"She went to town with Dad," I say. "And Macy and Jesse." I know I shouldn't lie but I don't know what else to do.

Mom's standing as still as a statue in the doorway, staring into the dark of our room. Then she slowly turns around and looks past me, to the front door. I'm scared she's going to go outside.

"Here, Mom, let me get your robe," I say,

backing up and reaching into her bedroom. Mom's still just standing there, so I hold her robe open. "It's your nice yellow one," I say.

Mom slowly raises one arm and puts it into the sleeve of her robe. I circle around back so she can get the other sleeve on, then I pull the shoulders up. She slowly reaches down for the belt, and ties it above her belly. Her hands slide down to rest on her belly again,

"Are you hungry, Mom?" I ask.

She doesn't look at me at first. Then when she does look at me she looks confused. And then she frowns.

"Anna?" I point toward the kitchen. "We have marmalade."

"Marmalade!" she says. "That's my favourite. What's yours?"

"I like jam," I say, leading her to the table. "Do you want some coffee?"

"Coffee's for grownups," she says. "I like milk."

We've done the puzzle twice. It's the sheep one today, which is a really easy one. Mom sings "Baa, baa, black sheep, have you any wool," which she knows all the words to. I got the dishes mostly done while she went to the bathroom. I'm waiting for her to go pee again so I can finish them.

We're starting the puzzle again when I see an ant crawling across the table.

"Look, Anna," I say. "An ant."

Mom leans down and looks at the ant. "Where's it going?" she asks.

The ant goes around the pile of puzzle pieces. "He might be looking for sugar."

"He?" Mom leans closer. "Is it a boy?"

"I'm not sure," I say. I wonder if there's a way to tell. The ant stops near the edge of the table, and I see there's a little bit of marmalade stuck there. "Look, it likes marmalade."

Mom laughs. "It's a marmalant," she says. "A marmalant, a marmalant. The ants go marching one by one, hurrah, hurrah," she sings. "The ants go marching one by one, hurrah, hurrah." She stands and picks up the puzzle lid. Using it for a drum, she marches around the table. "The ants go marching one by one, the little one stops to suck his thumb and they all go marching down, under the ground, round and round, boom, boom." She hands me the bottom of the puzzle box. "C'mon, you're up! The ants go marching two by two, hurrah, hurrah..."

I march beside her, thumping on the box, until we get to the end of the two-by-two part. Mom looks at the ant on the table. "Now your turn," she says. She tries to pick up the ant, but it runs away across the table. "Come play with us," she says, still trying to scoop it up. The ant scurries into the pile of puzzle pieces. "Hide and seek! Hide and seek!" Mom sits down and starts flipping the puzzle pieces right side up. "Come out, come out, wherever you are..."

It's almost eight-thirty. Dad and Macy should have been back by now. Mom looks happy playing hide and seek with the ant, so I get the dishtowel and finish drying the dishes. I'm just putting the last one away when I hear a truck coming down the driveway. It sounds like the lodge truck, and it pulls into the lodge parking spot. The doors slam, and there's footsteps on the porch. Mom looks up. "Good," she says. "More company. Did you bring us anything?"

"I brought you a hug," says Macy, hanging up her cap. She gives Mom a hug and goes to our room to put away her scarf and glasses.

"Drew," says Dad from the doorway. "Get on out here and give me a hand."

I get my cap and go out to help him do the chores.

Saturday, August 11

Mr. Blade's here. He came earlier than usual and Mom's still up, so Macy has to stay in the house to help her with the puzzle. Today it's the Saturday one with some fat bees on a big flower. But Dad says I should get down to the boathouse because the boats sure as hell aren't going to bail themselves. I'm glad I get to do this by myself because maybe there'll be a treasure left behind again. Like the Swiss army knife Jesse got. Before he went with the Forresters, he used it to make some stuff out of twigs and pieces of firewood. He said it was called whittling.

I thought maybe he'd made that word up, so the next time I was up in the shed I looked in the dictionary. I tried looking for witteling or wittle or wittel, but it wasn't on the wi pages. Then I thought maybe it would start out like the words when and white, so I tried the wh page, and there it was.

Whittle means two things. One is cut (shavings) from (wood, etc.) with a knife. I don't know what all those brackets are there for. The other thing whittle means is to shape or make by whittling:

to whittle a boat. That would take a lot of whit-tling, but I think what the dictionary means is a toy boat.

One of the things Jesse was working on was an airplane with extra wings. There was one pair of wings coming from the bottom of the plane and another coming from the top, right above the first pair. He called it a biplane. Not bye-plane as in it's going away, but bi as in two, for the two sets of wings. In the dictionary there's even a picture of one.

Jesse forgot to take the biplane with him. If I can find another Swiss army knife, I can finish it. Then if he comes back with the Forresters next summer, I'll give it to him for a surprise.

Jesse also made Macy a doll.

Macy used to have some dolls when we lived at Kelowna. Their bodies were smooth and they had hair. Some of them had eyes that opened and closed. Grandma used to give them to her for birthdays and at Christmas. But when we went to Platt's Landing, Dad said no way was he paying to move a bunch of crap when the place we were going to already had furniture. So I guess when the bank got our house, it also got all our toys and stuff. Except not some of our clothes, the ones we put in our school backpacks and took with us.

None of those clothes fit us any more. Well, actually, Jesse's stuff fits me. And Macy wears Mom's clothes, because now that Mom can't work the bank machine Dad says there's no point even trying to get her dressed. Mom's clothes are kind of big for Macy, but not much.

Jesse can't wear Dad's clothes yet, though. And Dad still needs his. So a couple of times Dad went to a something called a salvation army and got a couple of big bags of clothes. Some of them were the right size for Jesse, but most of them weren't. I wonder if the Forresters will take him to the salvation army to get some other clothes.

Maybe that salvation army is something like the Swiss army, the one that makes the knives.

I don't know if Macy liked the doll Jesse made her, or not. She looked like she was maybe going to cry when Jesse gave it to her, but she stopped herself. She put the doll in the safe place in back of the shed. So I think she wanted to keep it.

Then Jesse showed her what he made it with, the knife with all the blades and things. Macy said the twisty thing was called a corkscrew, and that it was for pulling the cork out of a wine bottle so you can pour out the wine.

Jesse thought that couldn't be right. Why would you need that on a knife? But we were up at the shed, so I got the dictionary and looked. Macy was right.

I get the tub and the rags out of the boat shed. It isn't locked because Dad already unlocked it this morning when he emptied the boathouse trashcan while we were making the garbage run. It didn't rain last night, but there was lots of water in boat number three. Dad says the damn thing must've sprung a leak, so if I know what's good for me I'll make sure it gets bailed at least three times a day.

This morning he wanted to get the garbage done before Mr. Blade came, so he didn't stop to clean out the boats. I climb into boat number one and check under the seats. There's no treasure, just a couple of candy bar wrappers. In boat number two there's some empty beer cans, and one full one. The seat's all sticky with something, too. I get one of the rags a bit wet and give it a good wipe. It smells like beer.

In boat number three there's no garbage or treasure, just lots of water. I get the scoop out from under the seat. The scoop used to be a plastic milk jug but the Cornells cut the top off it. It fits in the space between the side of the boat and the floorboards. There's a space under the floorboards for the water to go when it rains.

Once when some people caught some fish, they left them in the bottom of the boat. The water that was in there made one of the dead fish go under the floor boards. Then it really stunk something awful. Dad and Jesse had to pull the boat close to the shore and tip it to get the dead fish out, and then Jesse had to use some pine sol to make the smell go away.

I hope there aren't any dead fish in boat number four. When I finish bailing number three I carry the tub over to check. No treasure, no garbage, no fish. Just a little bit of water. Maybe number four has sprung a leak, too.

After I rinse the rag and hang it up to dry, I

put the garbage in the trash can beside the boat-house and haul the tub of beer cans to the lodge.

It sounds like Mr. Blade and Dad are still on the porch talking, so I don't go around front. I set the tub down and check on my ants. They're all hiding in their volcano. Or maybe they're out looking for food.

Dad's telling Mr. Blade the story of how he shot a deer a couple of weeks ago. It isn't the hunting season, so we're not supposed to tell any-one because you just never know when some bleeding heart environmentalist is going to get their panties into a twist.

I guess Dad is sure that Mr. Blade isn't one of the bleeding heart environmentalists.

He'd look funny in panties.

I almost laugh out loud.

I didn't like going in the shed while the deer was hanging in there. Good thing it was warm out, because after a couple of days Dad said the flies were getting to it and he and Jesse had to get it butchered right away. Macy wrapped the chunks of meat in some brown paper that was all shiny on one side which the Cornells had left in the lodge. My chore was to watch Mom and put the meat in the freezer in the office. That freezer looks like a fridge but it isn't. It's where we used to have ice for the guests. But Dad said that was too much trouble and he made a sign that says NO ICE and stuck that in the office window. Good thing, because I had to spread all the meat out on the freezer racks so it would freeze fast.

I wonder if ants eat meat. Maybe they're tired of sugar.

I get one of the empty beer cans and jiggle it. There's a little bit of beer still in it. I turn it upside down over the ant volcano, and a couple of drops fall into the dirt.

Two ants come out to take a look.

Mr. Blade says he'd best get his ass in gear. Dad goes into the house and comes back out. "Here, try some," he says. "Nice tender little doe. Doesn't get any better than this."

Mr. Blade laughs. "Yeah, well, I'll take your word for it, Jack. I got a few more stops to make. You best put that back in the freezer and bring me the cash."

"Yeah," says Dad. "About that. I'm a little short this month. Bookings are down, and we've had a couple cancellations and—"

"Jesus, Jack," says Mr. Blade.

Dad hates it when people interrupt him. But he doesn't say anything.

"When you gonna learn? The boss couldn't care less about your bookings, or your bookies, or any of your other goddamn excuses."

"Yeah, well you can't get blood from a stone," says Dad. "That's all I got. Maybe you could spot me the extra two hundred. I'll pay you back on the twenty-sixth."

Mr. Blade laughs. "Ain't gonna happen," he says. His footsteps go down the stairs and along the path. "You'd best enjoy them fingers while you got 'em." His car door closes. I wait while he backs it out of the parking place and goes up the driveway.

"Asshole," says Dad. The screen door slams, and I hurry to take in the tub.

Mom's gone to bed and Macy's cleaning the bathroom. Dad's in the office. The freezer door whacks shut.

I set the tub down and take the beer to the fridge. Dad comes out of the office and kicks the tub. "What the hell are these doing here?" Then he sees the beer I'm putting in the fridge. "Get those empties up to the compound," he says, crossing the kitchen to snatch the beer from my hand. He twists the gate key off his key ring and throws it in the tub. "I'll be up there in a minute to get started on the firewood."

He pops open the beer and turns around to stare out the window over the sink. I pick up the tub and skedaddle.

I dump the cans into the big bin and go into the shed for the axe. It might take Dad a few minutes to drink his beer, so I think about getting a Reader's Digest out of the hiding place. But then the fence makes a jingling noise. I pick up the splitting maul and hurry outside. It's Macy. The birds screech up out of the garbage pit when they see her coming, and she makes a face at them. "Stupid birds," she says. "Dad says he can't leave the office on a Saturday, so we're to do the firewood ourselves."

"Oh," I say. We go into the shed and I put away the splitting maul. It's too big for Macy to lift over her head. She picks up the axe and I get the hatchet. Outside the shed there are two big chunks of log called chopping blocks. Macy puts a smaller chunk of log, which is just called a block, up onto one of the chopping blocks. There's a split already starting in the block, and Macy turns the block so the split is pointing toward her. Then she swings the axe up over her head and lets it fall down onto the far side of the block. She's trying to make the axe come down so it makes a line with the split. This is how Dad showed us to chop firewood.

He says only an idiot wastes their energy doing it wrong.

Now comes the hard part. The axe is pretty heavy, so it's dug into the block and it doesn't want to let go. Macy has to push down and pull up on the handle, and it still doesn't budge.

"Gimme the hatchet for a sec," she says, and I hand it over.

She turns the hatchet upside down and hammers the flat part of it against the handle. I turn to look through the gate, down to the lodge.

"Don't worry," she says. "He won't leave Mom alone."

She gives the axe handle a couple more whacks and the axe head pops up. She hands me the hatchet, pulls the axe the rest of the way out of the block, and raises it up again. This time when it falls down, it makes a cracking noise instead of a thud. The block splits right in half and both pieces tumble to the ground.

Macy sets one half back on the chopping block and chops a thin slice off of it. She hands that to me, and I use the hatchet to cut most of it into skinny little sticks, which are called kindling. That's what we use to start the fire in the morning.

The guests use lots of kindling, too, in the cabins. Dad tried not giving them very much, but then they'd just come asking for more.

So I get to chop lots of kindling. When this piece is too little for me to hold without chopping off a finger, it goes with the rest of the firewood and I get another one.

Macy cuts the rest of the block into pieces, and then gets another one from the woodpile. "Drew," she says, "I think Mom's..." She sets the block onto the chopping block and looks at me. "I think Mom's pregnant."

"She can't be," I say. "The doctor told her she's not allowed to have babies any more."

"I know," says Macy, raising the axe. It comes down, thud, and it's stuck again. I hand her the hatchet. "The doctor told her no more babies after you were born."

I get another skinny piece of wood from the pile Macy's making. "Then how come she made Grace?"

Macy shrugs. "Grandma said Dad was only happy if Mom was barefoot and pregnant."

That's silly. Mom wore shoes. "Was Dad happy when Mom was pregnant?"

Macy swings the axe up again and lets it drop. It sticks in the block again, but this time when she wiggles it sideways the block makes a cracking noise and comes apart. "Dad's never been happy," she says.

"So how come Mom had kids?"

"Dad made her," says Macy. "Once when you were a baby he told Mom she was taking too long to get pregnant. He picked you up out of the highchair and said she probably didn't want kids, and he should just get some of us out of the way for her."

"Was he going to give me away?"

"Maybe. But I don't think so. He put his hand under your chin and made your face go red. You were crying and Mom said okay, okay."

I don't remember any of that. "And then what did he do?"

"He said it was too bad Daddy's little insurance policies were such a bunch of cry-babies. And then he told Mom it was time to hit the sack. Even though we hadn't had supper yet."

I think about this. "Was that after Dad went to the Deetocks farm?" I say.

She nods. I chop some more kindling.

I think I know how babies get made. I read some stuff in Reader's Digest about Jane's ovaries and something else she has that's called a womb. That's where babies grow. I think all women have them, in their bellies.

Maybe that's why Mom's belly is getting bigger while the rest of her is getting smaller.

The men help the women get a baby started by something called inseminating. I'm not sure how that part works, but Jesse told me they do it in the bedroom.

"Was that when they made Grace?" I ask.

Macy thinks about it for a moment. "I guess."

I get another piece of wood. "Macy," I say, "did Mom want Grace?"

Macy stops chopping and looks at me, frowning. "Of course she did," she says. "Mom loves Grace. She loves all of us."

But I wonder if she's right. Especially if Dad made her have us.

I never did get to tell Macy that Jesse and I were going to go and get Grace. But maybe if Mom does have another baby, she won't need Grace.

There's too much kindling around my chopping block now, so I gather it up and stack it alongside the shed. The roof hangs over it here and keeps it mostly dry when it rains. Macy's stacking the firewood up, too, except a couple of skinny pieces that are good for kindling. She tosses them over by my chopping block.

"Macy, do you like the doll Jesse made you?"

"Of course," she says.

"It's not as pretty as the ones from Grandma."

"I know," says Macy, twisting the axe out of the block and raising it again. "But it's the first time Jesse made one. Pretty good for a first try."

So I don't think she's mad at Jesse anymore.

Behind us, the birds are screeching again, and

a few of them fly right over our heads. Macy shakes her axe at them. She looks very fierce, and maybe she scares the birds because they flap away and don't come back.

"If I could fly, I'd go to the pyramids," I say.

"How about a castle?" says Macy.

"Or a castle," I say. "One with knights and dragons."

"You could be one of the knights," Macy says.

"Or the dragon," I tell her. "But I'd be the kind of dragon that can fly."

A loon call echoes up the lake. "Or maybe I'd be a loon."

"You're already loony," says Macy, and we laugh.

We keep chopping until Dad hollers up from the lodge that it's lunchtime.

Saturday, August 25

When I wake up, it's already light out. I hurry to get my clothes on and make my bed. Dad and Macy have to go to Vernon. That means it's my job to look after Mom. Maybe Macy forgot to wake me up. But when I come out of the bedroom, Macy's still here. She's standing in front of the washing machine.

"Isn't it the twenty-fifth?" I ask.

Macy nods. "When I got up, Dad was already gone," she says. She pours some soap into the machine. "Mom's gone too."

"Oh," I say. "Maybe Mom remembered how to use the bank machine."

Macy shakes her head. "I don't think so."

"Maybe she went to have the baby," I say.

"She wasn't big enough yet." She closes the lid and starting the machine.

"Maybe it's just a little baby?"

"Grace was pretty little when she was born," says Macy. "That's why she had to stay in the hospital so long. And Mom was way bigger than she is now. I think something's wrong." She raises the lid and points into the machine and points inside.

I look. The water's pink.

"What's that from?"

"There was blood on Mom's bed," she says. "Lots of it. I'm trying to remember last time that happened. I think it was when Mom lost a baby."

Mom lost a baby? I wonder where it was. "Did she find it?"

Macy looks funny at me. "No, I don't mean that kind of lost," she says. "Sometimes babies get born too early and they don't live and that's called losing a baby."

"Oh," I say. I read something about this. "A miscarriage."

Macy nods. She closes the lid and gets her cleaning supplies out of the closet. She puts some pine sol in one bucket and fills it up with cold water. "Are we out of hot water?" I ask. Once that happened and after that Dad started timing the showers.

"Cold's better for getting blood out," she says. I follow her into Mom's bedroom. There's blood on the mattress, and on the floor. Macy puts a dry rag on the blood on the mattress and tries to soak some of it up. She dumps the bloody rag into her empty bucket, wets a clean rag and starts wiping.

"Should I do the floor?" I ask. She nods.

It's after nine when we're done.

Macy's got the sheets into the dryer, and we're just starting to eat our toast when we hear the lodge truck come down the hill and stop, engine still running. I'm eating as fast as I can, but the dishes won't be done when Dad comes in.

But he doesn't even look. He just walks over to the bedroom, sticks his head in the door, and then looks at Macy. "Get that mattress propped up so's it'll dry," he says. "C'mon, Drew, we've got chores to do."

"Where's Mom?" Macy asks.

Dad's on his way out the front door. "Hospital," he says.

I stuff the rest of my toast into my mouth and hurry after him.

Saturdays and Sundays are the busiest days at the lodge. Mondays too, when it's a long week-end. Dad drives the lodge truck over to Cabin One. He gets the firewood and kindling out of the back of the truck and puts it beside the cabin.

I take a clean garbage bag out of the box in the cab and go over to the garbage can. Getting the garbage bag out is kind of tricky. You have to try not to spill it when it's full. This one's not very full, though. I tie the bag, and put the clean one in the can and put the lid back on. Then I put the garbage in the back of the truck.

We stop at Cabin Two and do the same thing, then at Cabin Three. Lots of days we can skip cabins because nobody's in them, but not usually on weekends.

We always have to stop at the boathouse, so

we do that next. I get the garbage, and Dad checks the boats. "You best get back down here and get number three bailed out," he says.

"I will," I say. I still haven't found a Swiss army knife, or anything else that's good.

Our last stop is at Cabin Four, and the garbage can here is overflowing so I take an extra bag with me. I manage to get the full bag out and tied, but I'm still picking up the garbage that's on the ground when Dad's done with the firewood. He picks up the full bag and tosses it in the truck. "Carry that up when you're done," he says, driving up the road to the compound.

I find a few more pieces of garbage in the bush alongside the road. There's some meat wrappers and an egg carton with the eggshells still stuck inside. Mom used to cook us eggs. I like scrambled the best. We got lots of them at Platt's Landing, because of the chickens. But Dad says they're too expensive to buy. There's some bones in the dirt, way past where the egg carton's lying. Maybe scavengers were here.

I'm still stuffing garbage into the bag when Dad passes me on his way back to the lodge. "We're low on kindling," he says. "Get some chopped. Macy'll be along shortly."

Up in the compound, the birds are already screaming at each other in the pit. When I throw in the bag of garbage, they flap up into the sky, make a couple of circles, and settle back down. Some of the crows start pecking into the new bag. The white birds are called seagulls.

They should be called lake-gulls instead.

Behind the shed there's an extra roof piece called a lean-to. That's where Dad parks the mower. If you get up on the roof of the lean-to, and you sit down, your head is almost as high as the roof of the shed. But if you sit just right, you're mostly hidden. That's where the shed's roof makes the back wall into a point.

In that pointy part of the wall, there's a hole that looks kind of like a little window with no glass. Jesse says it's called a vent. If you reach into the vent, you find our hiding place. The ceiling part of the shed is under the vent hole, so you can put stuff on top of it.

The roof leaks a bit, but mostly it keeps our stuff dry. So it's a good hiding spot.

The tricky part is getting up on the lean-to. You have to put your left foot up on top of the mower, and then put your right foot up onto the edge of the tool barrel, and then you grab the edge of the lean-to roof and pull yourself up. The lean-to shakes when you do this. But if you do it fast, it's not too scary.

You can even sit up there and listen for the loons and read because the trees make it a good hiding place. Except from the pit side, where somebody could see you. But nobody ever goes there except us, and Jesse said once he was up there when Dad came to dump some stuff in the pit, but he still didn't even see Jesse.

I guess people don't always look up.

Reader's Digest has this part about word

power, where you guess what the words mean. I'm figuring out word number six when the gate makes its jingly noise. It's probably Macy, but just in case I toss the magazine back through the vent and jump down off the lean-to. It sways a little and makes a bit of a creaking noise. I pretend I'm getting the pitchfork out of the barrel. Macy comes around the corner of the shed.

"Dad says you better be doing something useful," she says. "He can't hear any chopping."

We hurry to get the axe and the hatchet.

"Macy," I say, "how long does Mom have to stay in the hospital?"

She sighs, raising the axe. "She was gone for about three days when Grace was born," she says. "Dad got that Jennifer lady to come and stay with us because he was at work. And then when Mom came home, she had to go back to the hospital every day to see Grace. Also to get hooked up to some bags of stuff to make her healthy again. She had a thing stuck in her arm for them to plug the bags into."

"What about when I was born?" I ask.

"I don't really remember," she says.

"How about Jesse?"

She laughs. "I was only one year old."

I hope this baby is big enough to live. I wonder if it will be a boy or a girl. Maybe if it is a girl, then Mom will stop being sad about Grace.

But if she doesn't come back with a baby, maybe Macy will help me find Grace.

I hope Mom comes back soon.

It's quarter to nine and Macy's on her way to get her pajamas on when Dad says "Get your Anna outfit, Macy."

"Now?" says Macy.

I think Dad might whup her for that. But he's already on his way out the door.

Macy scurries to the bedroom and rummages in her suitcase. The truck's making the noise it makes when it doesn't want to start.

"Am I supposed to come, too?" I ask, trying not to block the light from the hall.

Macy rushes past me and grabs her cap. "I'll come and get you if he wants you," she says on her way out the door. The truck's running now. I hear it go into gear. Through the window in the front door, I watch the shine from the headlights go up the hill. Instead of going left, toward Lumby and Vernon, they go right.

That's the way to Cherryville. Dad never gets the cash there, because there's only one machine and it's too easy to watch. Also, he doesn't want Grandma's spies to know what neck of the woods we're in.

Dad hates Grandma's spies. One time, in Kelowna, Dad got the cash out of the machine himself. That's when one of Grandma's damn lawyers paid us a visit to make sure Mom was okay. Dad says Grandma's a high mucky muck so her spies get to look at the mug shots from the cash machines.

I guess that's why Macy has to dress like Mom when she gets the allowance.

But I don't think they have very good cameras if they think Macy is Mom. Or maybe they're not very good spies.

I think I might go in the office and get a newspaper out of the paper bin, but if I turn on the light someone might think the office is open. Sometimes people just knock on the door of the lodge and say they could see we're up because our lights are on, so could we get them something out of the store. Which is kind of dumb because the store doesn't have much in it, and besides it will be open in the morning. But Dad says most people are dumber than a sack of hammers. Which is pretty funny when you think about it.

But I don't want anyone to knock on the door while everybody's gone. Maybe I should turn off the kitchen light.

I turn the bathroom light on first so it won't be completely dark. Then I turn off the kitchen light and go in the bathroom. But what if a burglar comes in. I come back out of the bathroom and look to see if Macy locked the front door. She didn't. I think about going over there to lock it. But what if I'm part way there, and the door opens, and a burglar comes. Or one of the yahoo vandalizers that the Cornells were worried about. I listen for footsteps. I don't hear any, so I run to the front door and turn the lock. Then I listen again. The wind is blowing a little bit, and the lodge makes a creaking noise, like someone's sighing. I want to go back to the bathroom, where it's light.

I listen some more. The lodge sighs again. I decide this time I'm going to walk, really fast. As I go past the kitchen I see something moving on the other side of the table.

I run into the bathroom.

As I slam the door, I see something move above the toilet. That's where the window is.

Oh.

I slowly put my hand up over my head and see my hand's reflection waving back at me. There's a window on the other side of the table. The thing that moved in the kitchen was probably just my reflection, too.

I'm not taking any chances, though. I stay in the bathroom until I hear the lodge truck coming back down the driveway. Then I open the bathroom door, run to unlock the front door, and run for my bedroom.

I'm just pulling up the covers when Macy comes in. I want to ask her if everything went okay, but Dad doesn't like it when he hears whispering. So I pretend to be asleep.

Sunday, August 26

Sunday's checkout day, but also some people like to come and rent a boat to go fishing. We're finished the garbage run and now Dad's staying near the office. Macy's cleaning cabins and I'll have to do the laundry.

But it's also the twenty-sixth, and Dad will send me back outside when Mr. Blade comes. So I might be able to read for a while.

I think the leak in boat number three is worse. Good thing it's almost the end of the season. After the long weekend for Labour Day, which is next weekend, Dad will pull the boats back up to the compound. If the Cornells are still gone, maybe we'll stay here for another year. If we do, I hope Dad fixes the leak. He probably will because the guests that rented number three yesterday said the damn thing leaked like a sieve and they wanted their money back. And he needs all the money he can get to pay off the boss.

I want to get to the lodge before Mr. Blade comes, so Dad will send me back out. I can't tell if he's here yet. I've been listening, but the lake makes too much noise. There's the sloppy noise when the waves hit the boats, and a creaky noise when the boats rub the wharf, and the scrape and swoosh noise when I bail.

Finally I'm done.

There's nothing to haul up today, so I put the garbage in the trash can and the tub back into the boathouse, then I run up to the lodge.

Nobody's here yet.

Dad's in the office reading a newspaper. Sometimes people leave them in the cabins. I hope I'll get to read it, too, before he uses it to start the fire. Macy's brought a load of laundry up, so I load up the machine and put some soap in. Just before I start it, I hear a car coming down the drive. Maybe it's Mr. Blade.

It isn't. This man's taller than Mr. Blade. He has a shorter man with him. They walk right past the office window where Dad's sitting with his newspaper. They knock on the front door of the lodge. "Office is over here," Dad says.

The tall man stays in front of the door, but through the window I can see his head turn slowly toward the office window. "You were short on the eleventh, Mr. Sullivan," he says. "I prefer to conduct this kind of business behind closed doors."

I hear the office window slide shut, and Dad comes out of the office. He looks boiling mad, even more boiling than ever. He sees me by the washing machine. "Get out and help your sister," he says, opening the front door.

The two men outside stare at me through the screen, and for a minute I'm scared they won't let me out. Then the tall one steps aside and opens the screen door. "Let the kid out, Turk," he says. Turk steps back, and I think he might be laughing.

I make myself walk past him. But as soon as I get around the corner, I run.

Friday, September 7

Labour Day's over, so the gates at the top of the driveway are closed again, just like they were when we came here last September.

Dad's been pretty sick from drinking with the guests. And maybe from the painkillers. Last Sunday, one of the guests who checked out was a doctor. He gave Dad some painkillers for his hand, which had gotten hurt by the tall man and Turk. Dad told the doctor he hurt it himself by accidentally slamming the truck door on it. Which he didn't. But the doctor said it looked pretty busted up and Dad should really get in to the hospital to see about getting it set, which Macy says means the same as getting a cast like what Jesse had when he fell off his bike back in Kelowna.

I thought that would be a good idea and maybe Dad would take us to see Mom at the same time. But Dad didn't go to the hospital. And after two days the painkillers were all gone, but Dad's hand was still pretty bad. So when another doctor came on Friday for the long weekend, Dad used his charming voice to ask him if he happened to have any painkillers. This doctor was actually a dentist, but he had painkillers anyway. And he gave some to Dad and said not to drink any alcohol while he was taking them.

But then some other guests said for Dad to come have a few drinks with them and he did.

So maybe that's what made him sick. And when the young party punks from Vancouver checked out of Cabin One, they left lots of drinking stuff behind. Macy brought all of it up to the lodge, along with some from Cabin Four and a couple of beers from Cabin Three. So Dad had plenty of beer and other stuff to choose from.

On Wednesday morning Dad was feeling a bit better so he got the tractor going and covered up most of the dump pit. Then Macy and I helped him get all the boats back into the compound. The boats get put upside down on some sawhorses. When number three was upside down, you could see where the water was coming in. It's not really a hole. The wood there is just kind of soft and mushy like the wood on the roof of the lean-to.

After we helped with the boats, Dad and Macy went around with the truck and got the picnic tables from the cabins and from the boathouse. They had to make three trips because the tables took up too much room in the truck to do them all at once. Macy's pretty strong, and she can lift one end in and out of the truck without any help. The picnic tables get tipped up on their sides for the winter so the snow won't wreck them.

After the last trip Dad forgot to leave the truck running and then it didn't want to start. So Dad told Macy he wanted her to get in and crank the damn engine while he whacked the gas tank with a board, and he told me to get down to the lodge and get lunch started. But then he heard a truck stopping, and he looked at his watch and said the mail was here. So we all walked down to the lodge and Macy helped me open a can of soup and make some sandwiches.

While we did that, Dad walked up to the mailbox at the top of the driveway to see if his ship had come in. I guess it didn't, because he was pretty mad when he came back down. He didn't eat the soup I'd warmed up for him. He said he'd have some barley soup instead.

That isn't really soup, though. It's really beer.

Then yesterday, which was Thursday, Dad never even got out of bed except to pee and have another drink. It was pouring rain, so Macy and I made all seven of Mom's puzzles at least twice. I wanted to get a newspaper from the office but what if Dad came out and busted me for going in there. So I didn't.

This morning Dad's still in bed, but it isn't raining. So Macy and I are raking around the cabins. We had to climb over the gate to get the rakes, but the wheelbarrow is too big to push over the fence. So for now we're making piles.

And that's when I tell her how Jesse was going to help me find Grace so we could make Mom happy again.

"Were you two out of your minds?" she says. "Dad gave Grace away over a year ago. How would you find her?"

"We'd go to Mosquito Lake Lodge and look at their guest records," I say. "They have a book just like the one here. Then we'd phone the guests that were there when Dad gave her away."

"But do you even remember what day it was?"

"August twenty-seventh," I say.

Macy leans on her rake. "How were you going to get there?"

"Jesse was going to drive," I say. "At night, so people wouldn't see him because he's eleven."

"How were you going to get the truck?"

I already thought about this part. "We'd have to do it when he had lots to drink," I say. "We'd have sneaked into his room, got his keys, and snuck out. Then we'd drive up to Mosquito Lake Lodge, sneak into the lodge there, copy down the phone numbers, and sneak back. We'd put his keys back and go to bed and he'd never know."

Macy starts raking again. "What were you going to do with the phone numbers?" she asks. "Dad would know if you were using the phone."

"But by the time he got the bill, we'd have found Grace and Mom would get better. We'd get Mom to help us go get Grace and take all of us home to Kelowna. And Grandma would let us live with her."

Macy shakes her head. "You guys are crazy."

Then I tell her the best part. "What if Jesse's looking for Grace right now?"

Macy leans her rake against the cabin and sits down on the porch. "Jesse went away with the Forresters," she says.

"Yes, but maybe he told them about Grace. Maybe he got them to drive him up to Mosquito Lake Lodge. Maybe he's going to bring Grace here for a surprise."

Macy shakes her head. "Drew," she says, "Jesse's been gone for a month. Don't you think if he was going to look for Grace, he'd have brought her back by now?"

"Maybe," I say. "But maybe the people Dad gave Grace to are on vacation, so he's waiting for them to come back."

"Or Grandma," says Macy. "Maybe Jesse will go to Grandma and get her to help."

I never thought of that. I'm about to say that Grandma probably moved back to Europe, but Macy looks like she might be getting excited and I don't want to make her sad again. "Maybe," I say. "Macy, do you think Mom will help us go live with Grandma instead of Dad?"

As soon as I say it, I wish I had kept my big mouth shut.

But Macy doesn't look sad. She looks fierce. "Maybe," she says. "Then Dad could never give any of us away ever again."

We take the rakes back to the compound. Only a fool leaves tools lying around between jobs. There are just a couple of birds where the pit used to be, which makes Macy happy. Back at the lodge, Dad's still in bed so we make a couple of peanut butter and jam sandwiches and take them down to the boat wharf to eat them. It's kind of like a picnic. On the way back I show Macy where the ants used to live. I haven't seen any of them for a while.

"Maybe they're going dormant," she says while we're walking up to the compound to get the rakes. We've decided to rake around the boathouse next, and then Cabin Four.

"Do they do that?" I ask.

"I think so," she says. "Lots of insects hibernate for the winter. Is there something about ants in one of your magazines?"

"I don't know," I say. "Maybe, if Dad's still sleeping after we rake around Cabin Four, I'm going to go and see."

I'm up on the roof of the lean-to, flipping through my third Reader's Digest. The first two didn't have anything about ants, but I noticed a story about a man with a brain injury that I hadn't seen before, so I read that. When I hear the gate jingle I think it's probably just Macy, so I keep flipping. But it isn't Macy. It's Dad. He has a beer in his hand. He goes over to the lodge truck, opens the door, and sticks the key in the ignition. It makes a noise but it doesn't start. "Piece of shit," he says. Slamming the door. Maybe he won't notice me.

But then he does.

"What the hell are you doing up there?"

I can't think of what I should say.

"Get your ass down here!"

My legs won't move.

"Now," he says.

But my legs still won't move. Suddenly he pitches his beer can against the shed and comes running toward the lean-to.

Now my legs work. I stand and pull myself up onto the roof of the shed. Too late. The roof's still wet, and it's too slippery. I fall onto my bum.

Dad's cursing. I look over my shoulder. He's already on the tool barrel, pulling himself up on the lean-to. I crawl to the far edge of the roof, hold my breath, and jump into the nearest tree. I try to grab the first branch but I miss. I drop down to the next one, and I grab for it but I miss that one too. Then thud, I'm on the ground.

I get up and run. I run past Cabin Four, past the boathouse, past Cabin Three. I go past the road to the lodge, past the playground, past Cabin Two, past Cabin One to where the road ends and the walking trail starts. I run and run until I can't run any more, and then I turn around and look to see how soon Dad's going to catch me.

But Dad's not there.

What if he thought I went to the lodge? Macy's there. Dad's mad enough he'll whup her instead.

Should I go back and get him to chase me, so he'll leave her alone?

It's too late now. He'll already have her.

Maybe he won't hurt her too bad. But maybe if he sees me he'll get madder and whup her worse.

Maybe he didn't go to the lodge. Maybe he's hiding down the trail, waiting for me to come back. Then he'll jump out of the bushes and grab me.

I go off the walking trail and into the trees. I try to stay hidden from the trail, sneaking from tree to tree until I get close to where the playground is. I don't see Dad. And I can't hear anything from the lodge. Maybe he's already whupped Macy, and now he's having another drink and she's crying in our room.

Or maybe he's still hiding, waiting for me. If I wait until dark, I can sneak back to the lodge and see what's happening.

I sit down under a big tree, wrap my arms around my legs, and try not to cry.

It's dark. I'm so cold my teeth are chattering. My legs are stiff and it hurts to walk. Across the playground I can see the light in the window above the kitchen table. There's hardly any moon, so I have to try not to trip on the sandbox or run into the swings.

When I get closer to the lodge, I see somebody moving past the window. But it's too short to be Dad.

Macy must be okay.

If Dad is in there, he's going to whup me. But it's too cold to stay outside, so I go up the steps to the front door.

It's locked. I'm locked out.

I hear footsteps coming to the door. The curtain on the door window moves and Macy looks out at me. Then she unlocks the door and flings it open.

"Omigod, Drew," she says, grabbing me in a hug. "Where have you been? Where's Dad?"

She's crying, and I try to answer her but instead I start to cry, too. Macy closes the door. "Here," she says, going to the stove and dishing up some deer stew. "Eat something."

My teeth are still chattering. "I'm too cold."

"Okay," she says, dumping the stew back into the pot. "This'll wait. Go have a hot shower."

"But Dad—"

"It's hair night anyway," she says. She drags me into the bathroom. There's half a bottle of hair dye sitting on the counter. She grabs it, pulls off my cap, and starts rubbing the dye into my hair. I look at her in the mirror. Hers is already dark again, all the way to the roots. "I hope this stuff still works. He went to get you hours ago. Now, get in the shower."

"But it has to sit for—"

"Just keep your head out of the water for now," she says, rinsing her hands. "You're frozen stiff. You're lucky you're not dead of hypothermia. I'll drop your pajamas through the door once you're in." She switches on the fan, picks up the hair dye bottle and my cap, and goes out, closing the door behind her.

I turn on the water, strip down and climb in. At first it feels like it's burning, but pretty soon it feels kind of lukewarm so I turn up the heat a bit. I put the plug in the tub and sit down and turn the water to even warmer. After a while I quit shaking. Macy knocks on the door. She opens the door for a second. "You can rinse now," she says. I unplug the tub and let some of the water drain, then stick my head into the water and let the dye start to run out, then scrub some of it out with my fingers. I use a bit of shampoo to get the rest out so it won't stain my pillowcase.

When I'm done, I make sure there's no dye on the walls or the shower curtain or the tub. Then I shut off the water, squeegee the wet off the walls, and get a towel. Macy's left my pajamas just inside the door. I get them on and go to have my supper.

Dad's still not here. Maybe he's up drinking in the shed. Or one of the cabins. Maybe he let a guest come even though we're supposed to be closed for the season. Macy brings my bed blanket and puts it over my shoulders. I eat two bowls of stew and two pieces of toast while Macy puts on her pajamas and brushes her teeth.

Macy won't let me help her wash the dishes or clean up the kitchen. She says I have to go straight to bed to stay warm. In a few minutes, she climbs into her bed. "Night, Macy," I say.

"G'night, Drew," she says. "Have a good sleep."

Saturday, September 8

When I wake up it's already light out. I sit up and look at Macy's bed. She's still sleeping too, but then she wakes up.

"Omigod," she says. "What time is it?"

I have no idea, but I'm already out of bed and getting my clothes on. Macy grabs her clothes and hurries to the bathroom. I open the curtains. It's cloudy, and it looks like it's going to rain any minute. I make my bed and put my pajamas away. Macy comes back, stuffs her pajamas under her pillow and makes her bed.

"Did you see him?" I ask.

She shakes her head. I follow her out to the kitchen.

It's almost nine-thirty, even later than I thought. But Dad's not here. He's not in the bedroom, either. There's no dirty dishes, so he didn't come in and eat while we were sleeping.

"Maybe he drove to town while we were asleep," I say. "Maybe he went to get Mom and the new baby.

Macy shrugs. "Maybe," she says. She goes into the office and comes out with a piece of newspaper. "It's the classified section," she says, scrunching it up and stuffing it into the wood stove. "I left the rest of it there in case you get time to read it."

While she makes the fire, I get the toaster and put in a couple of slices of bread. I also fill up the kettle and plug it in, just in case Dad comes in and wants his coffee. But he doesn't. When the kettle whistles, Macy goes to the front door and peeks out the window. Then she goes to the closet where she keeps her cleaning supplies.

"Look," she says. "Hot chocolate."

I get out a couple of mugs and she spoons some of the chocolate powder into each. She puts the rest of the package in the cupboard with the coffee. Then she pours hot water into each cup and stirs it. I can hardly wait.

Macy has her toast with peanut butter and jam. I just have peanut butter. We're saving the marmalade for when Mom comes back. The hot chocolate tastes so good I want to have some more, but then it would be all gone.

After breakfast Macy and I do the dishes. Macy gets the hot chocolate and puts it back in her supply bucket. "If he sees it," she says, "I can say I forgot all about it."

After that we sweep the floor. I change the sheets on Mom and Dad's bed, and finish doing the laundry. Macy thinks it would be a good idea to clean the windows, so we do that, too. The Cornells are supposed to come back soon and then we need to find a new place to live. They are going to pay Dad for closing up, but only if he does it right. So the place has to look shipshape.

It's pouring rain outside, and besides we've done all the raking. We can't think of any other chores we need to do.

Macy opens the front door and looks at the rain. She closes the door again. "Wanna play Fish?"

"You have cards?"

She nods. They're in her cleaning supplies. "I've been saving them for a couple of weeks," she says.

"But what if Dad sees?"

She shrugs. "Maybe he won't burn them this time," she says. "Our chores are all done."

"Maybe we should just play tic tac toe," I say.

"We'd have to get the pencils and paper out of the office, so he'll be mad anyway," she says, dealing out seven cards each.

We play Fish, Crazy Eights, Snap, Old Maid and War. Then we put the cards away and make lunch.

After we do the dishes, Dad still isn't back so we get the cards out and play some more.

And we have some more hot chocolate, but we make sure we clean out our cups right away. There's still some left, so we put it back in with the cleaning stuff and get the cards out again. The rain keeps raining, Macy puts more wood in the fire, and we play some more cards.

It's the best day at Keneece ever.

Except I wish Jesse was here. And Mom and Grace. And the new baby, too.

Sunday, September 9

On Sunday we accidentally sleep in again. We have breakfast, clean up and play some cards while the sheets from Mom and Dad's bed are in the washer. It looks like it might rain, so we use the dryer instead of hanging them up. Macy puts her sheets in the washer.

At ten-thirty we drink the last of the hot chocolate. Then Macy says it would be a good idea to take the garbage out so Dad won't see we drank it. So I get a clean bag for the trashcan. It isn't raining any more, and we're both tired of being in the house. Macy decides she'll come with me to get rid of the garbage.

"If Dad went to get Mom, he'd be back by now," I say. "Maybe he's gone to look for a new place to live."

Macy thinks about this for a minute. "Maybe he already found a new place to live," she says. "Maybe he decided not to take us with him." She doesn't sound mad or sad or anything.

The compound gate is unlocked, and the lodge truck is still here. So Dad didn't go to town. Unless he hitchhiked.

The birds don't seem to care about the garbage pit now that it's mostly covered. But there's a bunch of them in back of the shed, squawking and flapping. I hope they're not fighting over my magazines. While Macy puts the garbage in the pit, I go over to have a look.

The tool barrel's knocked over, and the lean-to roof is lying on top of it, broken. I wonder if my magazines are still here, so I get the ladder out of the shed and take it around back.

Dad's jacket is lying there with the tools. One of the sleeves is kind of wrapped around the blade of the scythe, like the way he used to hold Jesse's neck when he was really mad.

And Dad's boots are there too.

Then I see what the birds are fighting over. It's not my magazines. It looks like the parts of the deer that Dad didn't want, the inside parts.

Except it's coming out of Dad.

Macy comes to see what I'm doing. "What's that smell?" she asks, looking over my shoulder. She walks closer to where Dad's jacket is, and then she stops. She turns around and runs past me, over to the far gate that leads out to where the Cornells' old dump used to be. She leans on the gate and pukes and pukes and pukes.

I wait a minute, and then go over to see if she's okay.

"Macy," I say, "is Dad dead?"

She nods and closes her eyes, leaning against the gate. "Drew, the other day when Dad came to get you, what happened?"

"I was on the lean-to," I say. "He said to get down, but I was too scared."

"Did he come after you?" she asks.

I nod.

And then I know what happened. The lean-to broke and Dad fell with the tools.

"It's all my fault," I say.

Macy opens her eyes and she just stares at me and I wonder if she'll be mad at me now.

"The police will put me in jail for killing him."

Macy starts to cry.

"I'm sorry," I say. "I didn't mean to."

Macy rubs her eyes. She looks over at the pit. "We'll bury him," she says, "and then nobody will ever know."

"Bury him?" I say.

She nods. "We have to get rid of the body," she says. "Like they do in the detective books."

I haven't read any detective books, but I shake my head. "That's not how you get rid of bodies," I say. "Mr. Blade told Dad you leave them out for the scavengers. After you strip them. You have to burn the clothes."

"Strip..." Macy looks over to where the birds are still squawking, then turns her head back to the gate and pukes again. She sinks down until she's sitting on the ground. She stares through the gate for a minute. Then she grabs at the gate and shakes it.

The next thing, she's climbing over it.

I come to follow her.

"Stay there," she says. She sounds really mad.

"Where are you—"

"Just stay there." She drops to the ground on the other side of the fence and reaches down into the grass. When she straightens up, she turns to look at me. She looks over to where the birds are, and then she turns and starts walking up the old dump road, fast. "Stay there," she says again.

After she goes a little ways I can't see her any more, so I climb over the gate and go after her. Around the corner, just past the tall tree, I catch up. She's going down the bank. It's really steep here. The rocks above the road have slid down and blocked it. Macy's climbing down the hill, making little rockslides that tumble toward the lake. Some of the rocks go all the way down and splash into the water.

Then Macy stops.

She grabs her belly and starts heaving again.

"Macy," I call.

A rock slides out from under my foot and bounces down the hill, almost hitting her.

She looks up at me.

"Stay there," she says. The rocks around her feet start to slide, and she grabs hold of a branch from the tall tree. Grabbing for another branch, she carefully climbs back up the bank.

"Are you okay?" I ask. Her hand is bleeding, and her eyes are all red.

"I'm okay."

We climb over the back gate and drop down into the compound. She starts toward the birds.

I hurry after her. "Don't go over there, Macy."

"I have to," she says. "We need the keys and his wallet."

"I can get them." I take her hand.

We walk over to where Dad's lying. Something small and dark and furry runs away, slinking under the fence. The birds scream at us, but then they go flapping up into the trees behind the shed.

The scythe blade has a reddish brown streak on it, and there's lots of reddish brown on Dad's jacket. I don't want to look at his head, so I'm glad his keys and wallet are in his jeans.

We'll have to roll him over somehow.

The pitchfork is mostly out of the barrel, so I pull it the rest of the way out. Macy uses it to push Dad's jacket further away from his front pocket, and I try not to see where the scavengers have been eating. I reach in to get the keys.

"Got them," I say.

The birds are still screaming. Macy pokes the pitchfork under Dad. We both lift on the handle until I can see Dad's back pocket, and Macy holds the pitchfork steady while I get the wallet out. Then Macy drops the pitchfork and runs down the hill to the lodge. As I follow her, I can hear the birds swooping down behind me.

That furry animal probably comes back too, but I don't look back to see.

Macy puts Dad's keys on the table and looks inside the wallet. There's five twenty-dollar bills, one five-dollar bill, and Mom's bank card. There's also Dad's driver's licence and a couple of other cards. One says CareCard. It has a flag on it. She sets them all out on the table.

I spin the keys around on the ring. There's the gate keys. One's for the two gates in the compound, and another's for the gates at the top of the hill. There's the keys for the cabins, and one for the boathouse. There's the truck key, and a little one that's for the mailbox at the top of the driveway.

"Macy," I say, "did Dad check the mail on Friday?"

Macy makes a frown. "I don't know," she says. She picks up the key ring, and we walk up to the top of the driveway where the mailbox is. The gate up here isn't like the one at the compound. Here, it's just a really long bar that goes across the driveway. I duck under it. Macy's legs are longer, so she kind of hop-steps over it.

Macy unlocks the mailbox. There are four envelopes inside. Macy locks the box and we go back down to the lodge.

One of the envelopes is blue. Macy lets me open that one. It's just junk mail. The other three are white. Two of them have lots of writing on the outside. One has a post office box number in Vernon, but that's crossed out and then there's the word "Forward" in big letters, and the address for Keneece Lake Resort. Macy opens that one.

I open another one of the white envelopes. It's

from the Cornells. After I finish reading it, I look to see what Macy's reading. "What's it say?"

Macy's finished reading the first page and she hands it to me. It's a letter from Grandma to Mom. Grandma says she's out of her mind with worry, and she really, really wants Mom to call her. Macy's done the second page.

"We should call Grandma right away," I say. "Maybe we can go live with her until Mom's out of the hospital."

Macy shakes her head. "Grandma is living in a care home," she says. "We can't live with her."

"Well, she could send her driver for us, though. And he could take us to see Mom."

Macy bites her lip. "Maybe," she says. "The number for the home is right here. But if we can't live with Grandma, and Mom's in the hospital..."

"And they might put me in jail, too," I say.

Macy looks at me. "Drew, it was an accident. You didn't push Dad or hit him, did you?"

I shake my head.

"Well, then, it wasn't your fault," she says.

"But what if the police think I did push him?"

Macy looks at the letter from the Cornells. "What's that one say?"

I push the letter over to her. "The Cornells are coming back," I tell her. "They said if we can't wait until they get here, we should just lock everything up and leave the keys in the mailbox. They have an extra one. And if everything's in good shape, they'll mail Dad a cheque."

"When are they coming?"

I point to that part in the letter. "Late on the fifteenth," I say.

Macy looks at the calendar. "Today's the ninth. The day after tomorrow, Mr. Blade will come."

I get a sick feeling in my stomach. "Or the tall man and Turk."

Macy looks at her hands. "Drew, we have to get the allowance."

"We can get it at Cherryville," I say, "and then go up to Mosquito Lake and find out the guests that were there when Dad gave Grace away. And then we'll come back here and call people until we find her. And we can call Grandma and she can get her driver to get us, and then he take us to get Grace."

"How will we get to Mosquito Lake?"

"You can drive," I say.

"I only drove the truck once," she says.

"You can do it," I tell her.

"We should just get Grandma's driver to take us to Mosquito Lake," she says. She picks up Grandma's letter, and I follow her into the office. She lifts the phone and puts it to her ear. Then she sets it back down.

"It's dead," she says.

"Oh," I say.

"Drew, Mosquito Lake will be vacant. What if we just use their phone to find Grace?"

I look at my fingers. "Do you think Mr. Blade will catch us?"

"The bagmen won't be looking for us there," she says. "Let's just leave this place and never come back."

I think about it. If we get Grace back and take her to Mom at the hospital and call the Forresters, we could be a real family again.

Macy puts the money and the bank card in her pocket. Then she gets Mom's suitcase. She puts all of Dad's stuff in some garbage bags.

I put Macy's sheets in the dryer and start mine washing, and then I go and make Mom and Dad's bed.

Macy writes a note for the Cornells to let them know the beds are clean, and that she's sorry about the accident that happened up at the compound and that they should call the police and make sure to tell them it really wasn't anyone's fault. And that we are very sorry to borrow the truck without asking but we will get Grandma's driver to bring it back to them as soon as we can.

I write a note for Jesse to tell him we're going to find Grace in case he hasn't already done that, and that Mom's at the hospital and Grandma's in the care home, and that he should call her right away and then we'll be a family. I get an envelope from the office and copy the Forresters' address from the client files.

I put my sheets in the dryer and we make a loaf of bread into sandwiches. We eat two of the sandwiches and drink the last of the milk. Then we take all the garbage and the bags of Dad's stuff up to the dump. Macy tries her best to ignore the birds. She gets into the truck, puts in the key, and squishes her lips together tight.

The truck starts.

Macy holds the steering wheel really tight and rolls the truck out of the compound. She leaves it running while we close the gate and lock it, and then when we stop by the lodge to get Mom's suitcase and Macy's suitcase and my backpack, and the rest of the sandwiches. I put the letter for Jesse in my pocket.

Macy gets the key ring off the truck key without shutting it off. She locks the lodge, then hands me the key ring. I walk up to the top of the driveway to undo the padlock on the big bar, and swing it open.

Macy gets the truck to go slowly up the hill. At the top she almost scrapes it against the gate post, but she misses it. Then she goes too far out onto the road but it's okay because no one is ever coming anyway. And then when she turns right she gets it to not go in the ditch.

I close the road gate and lock it. Then I open the mailbox and put the key ring inside.

"Ready?" I call.

Macy doesn't turn to look at me but she nods, still holding tight to the wheel.

I close the mailbox and it locks shut. Then I climb into the truck and put on my seatbelt.

This lodge truck isn't like the one at Mosquito Lake. That one was even hard for Mom to drive because it had an extra pedal, called a clutch. But Macy's never driven on Creighton Valley

Road before, and I can tell she's scared. I'm scared, too. The lake's on my side, and Macy tries to keep the truck pretty far away from the edge of the road, but sometimes she makes it go too close.

I stop looking out my side window.

Pretty soon we're past the lake, but the drop from the side of the road is still steep, and there's lots of corners. After a couple of miles Macy seems to be getting the hang of it a bit better. But then we get to the first hairpin corner.

A hairpin corner's where the road's going one way and then it turns so that suddenly you're going back the way you came. The road here is on a steep hill, too, so the truck wants to go fast. Macy uses the gearshift to make it go slower like Dad does coming down the driveway. But it's still not slow enough, so she pushes on the brake pedal. She's almost standing up on it, and her hands are wrapped around the steering wheel, and her knuckles are all white.

We get around the corner okay and Macy sits back down on the seat. We crawl along for a few minutes, and then there's the other hairpin. This time we're going too fast, and we go really close to the edge on Macy's side. Then we go really close to the edge on my side. Macy stands right up again.

Then she finally gets the truck to go the way she wants it.

Tears are running down her face and dripping off her chin.

"Maybe in Cherryville we should call Grandma," I say. "Her driver can take us to Mosquito Lake."

"Drew, nobody's going to help us break in at Mosquito Lake," says Macy. She sounds really mad.

The truck goes way over on her side again, and then way over on my side. Macy's sobbing.

"Well, we could call the Forresters," I say. "Jesse could drive us up to Mosquito Lake."

Macy stands up on the brakes again, even though we're on a straight stretch now. She slams the gearshift into the P for park and smacks the steering wheel. "Jesse can't help us," she screams. "Will you just shut up about him?"

Now I start to cry. "I just thought..."

Macy digs into her pocket and pulls out a Swiss army knife. It's just like the one Jesse had. "Look!" she yells. "This was by the back gate of the compound. Jesse lost it going over the back fence."

"Oh," I say.

"You know what the birds did to Dad?" Macy throws the knife on the floor by my feet. "Well they did it to Jesse first." She's sobbing and hitting the steering wheel with her fist. "Up the old dump road, by the tall tree, down the bank. Where Dad threw all the deer bones. I found him..." She hiccups, and her voice goes quieter. "I found him..." She puts her head down on the steering wheel and sobs.

Tears start running down my face too.

I look out my window. Here, the bank goes

straight up instead of straight down. But in the ditch there's a little stream with some green stuff growing.

I use my sleeve to get the tears off my chin.

Macy's crying is quieter now. She rubs her eyes, hard. Then she puts the gearshift on the number two and takes her foot of the brake. I reach down beside the suitcase and pick up the knife.

It's starting to get dark when we see the sign for the bible camp. There's another sign that says it's closed for the season. Macy stops the truck and we look at the camp. It has a couple of cabins and a barn. There's no lights on, and no smoke coming from the chimneys. Macy carefully turns the truck into the driveway. She drives around back of the biggest building, puts the gearshift in park, and shuts off the engine.

We eat a couple of the sandwiches. The little stream that's been running alongside the road goes through here, too, and even though it's pretty dark we get out of the truck to rinse our hands and have a drink. The water's really cold, and it's cold inside the truck now, too. I wish we'd brought one of the blankets from Keneece, but Macy was right. It was bad enough we were stealing their truck.

Macy's really quiet, and I don't want to say anything to make her cry again. So I just tell her goodnight. She puts her arm over my shoulders and pulls me along the truck seat so we're closer together. "G'night, Drew," she says.

I wake up a little while later. I'm really cold, and I can tell Macy is, too. She has piled all our clothes on top of us, but she's shivering.

"Macy," I say," do you think there's blankets in the cabins?"

She nods. We stuff our clothes back in the suitcase and get out, and she locks the truck and puts the key in her pocket. There's just a little bit of moon, enough to see the steps to the cabin. Macy tries the door, but it's locked. It has a deadbolt like the one at Keneece. There's a window in the door, too. Macy goes back down the steps and feels around on the ground. She comes back with a rock, and smashes a hole in the window. Then she reaches in and turns the bolt.

The cabin has electric lights and a wood stove. Macy finds some matches and some paper and some firewood, but no kindling. I use Jesse's knife to cut some shavings from a piece of wood, and Macy gets the fire going.

There's a bed, but no blankets on it. But there's some heavy curtains on the window. Macy takes the rod down and pulls the curtains off. They're kind of dusty. She takes them outside and shakes them. When she comes back she stuffs some newspaper into the hole in the window.

I look at the posters on the wall above the stove. Jesus loves you. We are all God's children.

I remember Grandma telling us some stuff about God and Jesus and heaven and hell.

When the fire's strong enough, Macy puts some more wood in and closes the vent so it won't burn too hot. She turns off the light, but a bit of firelight still flickers from the stove and it lights up the words on the wall.

We take off our shoes and curl up on the mattress. Macy pulls the curtains over top of us.

"Macy," I say, "do you think we'll go to hell for breaking in?"

"We'll come back and pay for the window, after we find Grace."

So I guess we're still going to Mosquito Lake. Even though Jesse's dead.

I hope Grace isn't.

"Macy," I say, "do you think..."

She puts her hand over my mouth.

I think maybe she's crying.

Monday, September 10

I wake up starving. Macy and I eat a couple of the sandwiches. Then we hang the curtains back up. There's a pencil hanging beside the calendar. Macy gets a piece of paper from the wood-box and writes a note to the church camp people to say sorry about the window, and we'll come back to pay for it as soon as we can. She leaves the note on the table.

Then we're ready to go.

She pulls the newspaper out of the hole in the window. We go outside and she reaches in to lock the door. Then she stuffs the newspaper back into the hole. We get into the truck and put on our seatbelts.

Macy takes a big breath. She puts the key in and turns it, but it makes the noise that says it isn't going to start. She turns the key again and the engine makes the same noise. She tries a few more times.

"Drew," she says, "remember when the truck wouldn't start and Dad was going to bang on the fuel tank?"

I nod.

"Did you see where Dad was going to hit?"

I nod again and unbuckle my seatbelt. I don't see any flat wood like Dad was going to use, but the rock Macy broke the window with was kind of flat. I go and get it. Then I go around the truck and stand about where Dad was standing.

"Ready," I say.

Macy turns the key and I bang a few times on the place where I think Dad was going to hit. But nothing happens. It keeps making the same noise. After a while the noise gets slower and slower and slower. And then it doesn't even make that noise anymore.

I drop the rock and go over by the door of the truck.

Macy slides out. She takes off her cap and looks up at the sky. I don't know if she's mad or sad or what, so I don't say anything.

After a bit, Macy reaches for her suitcase. She gets out Mom's scarf and sunglasses and a sweatshirt. "Drew, can we share your backpack?"

"Sure," I say. I go around the truck and get it.

Macy takes my clothes out and wedges them into her suitcase, all except one sweatshirt, which she puts back into the backpack with her own sweatshirt and the scarf and glasses. "Can you grab the rest of the sandwiches, too? And lock your side of the truck."

She closes up her suitcase and leaves it on the floor of the lodge truck. Then she locks the door. I give her the sandwiches, she puts them in the backpack and zips it up.

We start walking toward the road. "Macy," I say, "when we get to Cherryville, maybe we should just go to Vernon and find Mom."

Macy shakes her head. "Not until we find Grace."

It's good that it's a sunny day. Pretty soon I want to take my jacket off, but Macy's already carrying everything in my backpack. But after a while she takes her jacket off and ties it around her like a belt. So that's what I do, too. Then we see a driveway, and after a bit there's a house and a barn. And then there's a couple more houses, closer together. One of them has a bunch of stuff in the yard. There's balloons tied to the gate, with a sign that says "Yard Sale All Week."

Macy stops, looking at the stuff in the yard.

"Drew, look at those bicycles," she says, pointing. "We could get to Mosquito Lake a lot faster if we're riding."

I get a kind of sick feeling in my stomach as I follow her down the driveway. There's a dog lying on the porch, and he barks at us but he doesn't get up.

"Is it hard?" I ask.

She stops and looks at me.

"Riding a bike," I say. "Is it hard?"

"I forgot," she says. "You never did it."

The door opens and a woman looks out at us. "Well, hello," she says. "Say, why aren't you kids in school?"

"We're home schooled," says Macy.

"Then you must be the Larsens' grandkids

here for a visit," says the woman. "How nice. Well, now, are you interested in the bikes? We got one that'll fit your brother, and another one that's big enough for you. That one comes with a tow trailer, if you want it."

Macy goes over to take a look at the trailer. "My brother hasn't learned to ride yet," she says. "How much for the bike and the trailer?"

"Hundred twenty-five bucks," says the woman, watching Macy's face. "But I might be able to let you have it for a hundred. You got that much vacation money burning a hole in your pocket?"

I wonder what vacation money means, and how it catches fire. I'll ask Macy later. Right now she's looking at the trailer. It has a cover that comes up, kind of like a little tent. The woman unzips the cover. "Look here," she says. "Big enough for your brother to ride in. Why don't you take 'er for a spin?"

Macy looks at me, and raises her eyebrows. "Wanna try it?" she asks.

I'm not sure. The trailer has a little seat in it, and a clear plastic window you can look out of. Macy looks like she wants it.

I guess it can't be any more dangerous than riding in the truck with her driving. And it's a long walk to Mosquito Lake.

It's been a few years since Macy's been on a bike, and I think she might have forgot how. But then I remember that Jesse went riding with the Forresters after he hadn't been on a bike for years. So I guess it'll be alright.

I climb in.

"It's a ladies' bike," says the woman, "so you won't have any trouble with that. Nice twelve-speed. Used to use it for grocery-gettin', but my knees can't take the peddlin' no more. Take 'er up the drive and see what you think."

Macy takes off her jacket and hands it to me, then she gets on. She pedals up the driveway, wobbling a bit but not much. Out in the road she turns the bike back around and rides it back. It's not scary at all.

The woman's smiling at us. "Whaddya think?" she says. "Look, for a hundred ten, I'll even throw in the helmet. Ain't got one for your brother, but there's an old hockey helmet around here somewheres that'll do."

Macy climbs off the bike, shaking her head. "I only have a hundred and five," she says, "and we need some of that for groceries, too."

The woman frowns. I tug at Macy's sleeve. "We can use the allowance," I say.

"But there's only one bank machine," she says. "What if it's not working?"

"Oh, honey, don' you worry 'bout that," says the woman. "There's two, one at the Short Stop and another over at the Watering Hole Pub. An' if they're both down, Elma at the Short Stop'll let you get your groceries with debit." She's looking at Macy. "Hundred and five, and I'll throw in that Superman sleepin' bag your brother's admirin'."

But we can't go in the pub, so what if the cash machine at the Short Stop doesn't work?

Also, Dad says never to buy anything with plastic because it leaves a trail, and by that he means don't use the debit card to pay for stuff.

So I think Macy will say no.

But she gets all the money out of her pocket and gives it to the woman.

"Nice doin' business with you," says the woman, counting the money. She gets the bike helmet and Macy looks a bit scared for a minute, but then she takes off her cap. The woman makes a funny face at her hair, but then she smiles. Good thing it's only been a couple of days since we put the hair dye on.

She helps Macy wiggle the straps until they fit right, and then she helps me with the hockey helmet. It kind of stinks, but I don't want to say anything.

Macy climbs onto the bike. I get into the trailer and the woman hands me the Superman sleeping bag, then she zips the trailer closed. "Tell yer Grandma that Betty down the road says hi," she says.

When I look back at her through the window, she's waving at us. So I wave back.

It's kind of nice riding in the trailer. After a bit it kind of warms up, and I see that there's a screen on one of the windows and an extra zipper which opens just the plastic part. It lets fresh air in, but also some dust. Then we get on the pavement part of the road. Macy goes a bit faster. She seems to be doing okay with riding the bike, and pretty soon we get to the highway. Mosquito Lake's to the right, but Macy goes left toward Cherryville.

When we get to the Short Stop, Macy rides past it. I wonder what she's doing. There's a sign in the window that says open, but sometimes people in stores just forget to turn those signs off. But there's also a red pick-up truck right outside, and across the parking lot, next to the road, there's a big black SUV like the one the tall man and Turk were driving. Maybe it's them. So maybe that's why she doesn't want to stop here.

Macy goes a bit further down the highway and then turns right. Then she turns left. There's an old building here with a big sign that says The Watering Hole.

Macy stops the bike and takes off her helmet. She's smiling really big. I climb out of the trailer and undo my helmet. Under my chin is itchy. Macy's scratching under hers, too.

"Well," she says, "what did you think?"

"I like it," I say.

She reaches for the backpack. "Can you stay with the bike while I go in and get the money?"

I can't believe Macy's going to go into the pub. Even with Mom's scarf and glasses, people will know she's still a kid. "But you can't. You're not a grownup."

"This is where Dad brought me last time," she says. Even though she's all sweaty from riding the bike, she's putting on her jacket. "There was a closed sign at the Short Stop that said to use the machine over here. Dad was mad that he'd have to get the money himself, but it turned out the machine's out in the front porch part of the pub, before you go all the way in."

"Oh," I say.

I don't really want to wait by myself. But Macy is already going up the steps.

She comes back out in a minute, zipping up her jacket pocket. Then she takes off her jacket and hands it to me. "Stuff this in the backpack," she says. She starts to hand me the scarf and glasses, too, and then she looks at them. "I don't think I want to use these any more," she says.

She goes back up the steps onto the porch, and drops the glasses and the scarf in the trash.

We take the back way to the Short Stop, and Macy parks alongside the building, next to the washrooms. There's a sign that says the keys are at the desk. We put on our caps, leave our helmets and the Superman sleeping bag in the trailer, and go around to the steps.

The black SUV is still there.

Macy asks the woman behind the counter for the keys to the washrooms.

"Here's the one for the ladies," she says. "Men's is occupied. Just get it from the fella when he comes out."

We go back out and Macy unlocks the ladies room. I stay near the men's room door. I was hungry, but now my stomach feels kind of sick.

What if that's the tall man in there, or Turk?

But it isn't. The man that comes out is wearing the same kind of clothes as them, though. It's called a suit. Dad had to wear one of those once, before he went to the Deetocks' farm, when he went someplace else called the court.

The man holds the door open. "Next," he says. But he doesn't give me the key. I hope he's taking it back in the store. What if he doesn't. What if he's working for the boss and he uses the key and he comes in and asks for the money. But inside the washroom there's one of those sliding bolt things that doesn't use the key, so I slide it over. Then I go pee.

After I wash my hands, I wait until I hear Macy open the door to the ladies'. Then I slide the bolt back and come out of the washroom.

The man from the washroom is in the Short Stop, too. He's buying a coffee, but when he goes to pay for it he jumps a little. He pulls a phone out of his pocket. "Hello?" he says. "Hello? Hello?"

The woman at the counter puts his money in the till. "There's a better signal out by the high-way," she says.

The man leaves his coffee on the counter and hurries outside.

Macy's at the back of the store getting a small bottle of milk out of the big glass fridge. She hands it to me and gets a box of graham crackers and a small jar of peanut butter.

The man in the suit comes running back into the store. "Is there another ATM here?" he asks.

"Yeah," says the woman. "At the Watering Hole. Down the side road here, then right for a couple blocks."

The man rushes back out. His coffee's still on the counter and I wonder if he'll come back for it. I look outside, and the black SUV is driving fast through the parking lot.

Macy's at the till, getting two apples and two bananas out of a basket. The woman starts ringing them up. "Hey, I haven't seen you two in here before. You're not with the family that guy's looking for, are you? Four kids? He gave me a poster and everything."

"We're visiting our grandparents," says Macy. She takes a twenty dollar bill from her jeans and passes it to the woman.

"Oh, you must be the Larsens' grandkids," says the woman. "Say hi to them for me."

"We will," says Macy. She picks up the bag of groceries and we go back out to the bike. We open our milk and share it, and eat a couple of the crackers, dipping them in the peanut butter. Then Macy goes over to where the payphone is and starts reading the instructions.

She gets out the change the woman gave her, and counts it. There's a phone book hanging beside it, and she opens it up. "Drew, there's a number here for the hospital in Vernon."

I come over to stand beside her.

She puts some money into the phone and then pushes the buttons. I hear some ringing noises, then a voice.

Macy looks at me. "Umm, I'm Anna Sullivan's daughter, Macy," she says.

The voice on the phone says something I can't really hear.

"Umm, she came in couple of weeks ago," says Macy. The voice says something else.

"I think she was going to have a baby," says Macy. "Please, she's our mom and we're trying to find her."

The voice says something short, and then it's quiet for a bit. Then the voice comes back and says something else.

"Oh," says Macy. The voice says something else. "No, I... no, I'll try to find my grandma," she says. The voice is still talking but Macy hangs up the phone. She looks at me.

There's a squealing noise down the street. A pick-up truck honks its horn and the driver is shaking his fist at the man driving the black SUV. It looks like he didn't stop at the stop sign. I tug at Macy's sleeve.

"Macy," I say, "what if he's the new Mr. Bagman."

The SUV screeches into the parking lot, and the man in the suit rolls down his window. For a second I think he's going to talk to us, but then I see the woman from the Short Stop is outside with her broom.

"Hey," says the man. "Where's that place you thought they might be?"

The woman points up the highway with her broom. "Keneece Lake," she says. "About seven, eight miles up Creighton Valley Road, which goes off to your right just up that way. But that's a family of three kids, not four." The man in the suit is already driving away.

Macy looks at me. "But it's not the eleventh until tomorrow," she says.

"Maybe because Dad was short?" I say.

"We better go," she says, strapping on her helmet.

By the time I get mine done up, she's already pedalled us out onto the highway.

Finally, we're heading for Mosquito Lake.

It's kind of dangerous on the highway because every few minutes a car or a truck goes by, and they're going pretty fast. On the corners they sometimes screech as they go around us. And when the big trucks go by it feels like their wind is going to blow us into the ditch.

Macy's getting tuckered out from pedalling uphill, so I get out to make the trailer lighter. We're pretty far past the turn-off to Creighton Valley Road, but we're still a long way from Mosquito Lake. Macy wants to get there before it gets dark, but she says we probably won't.

Then a car slows down right beside us. The woman riding in the front seat rolls down her window. "Hey," she says, "do you know four kids from Keneece Lake?"

Macy shakes her head. "Sorry, no," she says, still pedaling. Her voice sounds like she's all out of breath. "We just got here. We're visiting our grandparents."

The car creeps along beside us, and the driver says something and hands the woman a piece of paper. "Bill, it's not them," she says. Then she peers at me. "Well, maybe... Can you take off your helmets?"

I look at Macy. We shouldn't be talking to grownups, but we're not supposed to argue with them either. She stops, unbuckles her helmet and pulls it off, so I start undoing mine.

"Oh, never mind," says the woman. "Bill, these aren't the kids he's looking for. Honestly, we'll be lucky not to get in trouble for..." she turns to us. "Sorry," she says, rolling up the window. "You kids ride safe, now." The car pulls away.

Macy looks at the bike. "Maybe we should be walking in the bush, instead," she says.

The bushes on the other side of the ditch look pretty thick.

"How much farther?" I ask.

Macy shakes her head. "Too far for today," she says. "And it's going to get dark soon. We'd better start looking for someplace to spend the night."

"We can both fit in the trailer," I say, "and we have the Superman sleeping bag."

Macy smiles. We've come to a place where the road's kind of flat again. "Climb in," she says. "Keep an eye out for a good place to pull off."

After a long time, only a couple more cars go by, and another big truck. Nobody seems to notice us.

Maybe Macy's wrong, and we will get to Mosquito Lake before dark.

And then we'll go and find the guest records, and we'll look for the guests that were there the night Dad gave Grace away. And then we'll start phoning them. We might even use the phone right there at Mosquito Lake. Maybe, in just a couple more hours, we'll find Grace.

And then we'll phone Grandma and get her driver to come and get us. And he'll drive with us to where Grace is, and then we'll all go see Mom.

And then everything will be perfect.

I might have fallen asleep, because all of a sudden it's dark. Macy's not riding the bike, she's walking beside it again, pushing it up the hill.

"I'll get out, Macy," I call.

She stops and I unzip the trailer door. "I'm sorry," I tell her.

"That's okay," she says. "You were sleeping."

Then I notice we're on a dirt road. "Where are we?" I ask.

She smiles. "Mosquito Lake," she says. "We made it."

The road into Mosquito Lake is a few miles long. I look behind me and see the highway. Maybe I woke up when we bumped off the pavement.

"Hungry?" Macy asks.

"A bit," I say. We get the groceries out. Macy's shivering, and we put on our sweatshirts and Macy puts on her jacket. Then she sits beside me in the trailer. We finish the milk and eat the apples, and have some more crackers and peanut butter. I wish we had some hot chocolate, or some soup. Macy unrolls the sleeping bag and puts it over our legs.

When she's done eating, Macy gets out. "I can't see to ride the bike," she says. "I'll have to walk. Want to ride in the trailer?"

I shake my head. I'm so excited I can't sit still. I'd rather walk. Actually, I want to run.

There's only a tiny bit of moon, and where the trees are really tall it's kind of spooky. But not too bad. And pretty soon instead of tall trees, there's lots of open space where you can see the stars. And then there's lots more open space and we can see the lake, across the grass over to our left. And over to our right, where there's still lots of trees, there's Mosquito Creek Lodge.

Macy stops the bike and we just stand there for a moment and look at the lodge. Then she takes my hand. We cross the empty parking lot and go up the steps. I can barely make out the sign on the door that says Closed for the Season.

The door's locked, but Macy reaches around in the flowerpot to find the key Mr. Thompson keeps there. She unlocks the door, and we go in.

The lights in the porch work. Macy goes across the kitchen to turn on the big light, and that's when it happens. The bedroom door flies open, and there's a man standing there.

"What the hell?" he yells.

"Run!" says Macy.

The man turns toward where she is, but she's already running around the table and heading for the door.

I run out the door and scramble down to the river. I can hear Macy behind me. I run through the dark, heading for the rotten old footbridge, and suddenly I'm tumbling down the hill. Then I'm in the water. It's so cold I can't breathe. The water tumbles me a bit more, but then I bump up against something.

It feels like a branch. I hold onto it while I get some breath, but I'm so cold my lungs won't work. I try to stand up, and my feet slip and slide on the big round river rocks. The darkness on one side of me is blacker than on the other, so it's probably the riverbank. I pull my way along the branch and up onto the ground.

I try to listen for Macy, but the river roars too loud, and the only other thing I hear is a pounding in my ears. I move as far as I can from the river, but the bank is too steep to climb. I sit down and pull my legs up against my chest.

I want to call Macy, but what if the man hears me. And then if Macy comes, he'll get both of us.

So I wait.

I'll look for Macy when it's light out.

I pull my legs closer and rock back and forth. I can't feel my feet, or my fingers. Riding in the trailer, it was nice and warm. That Superman sleeping bag would be perfect right now, but I'm pretty sure I'm on the wrong side of the river to go and get it. Maybe Macy got back to the bike and she's using it. I hope so.

I try to sleep so the time will go faster, but at first it's too cold.

But after a bit, it isn't so cold anymore. And then it's warm. Then I see why. I'm not down by the river after all. I'm on a little hill, and the sun's coming up, and the sky is the colour of marmalade. And when I look down the grassy hill I see the best thing I've ever seen in my whole entire life. Mom's walking toward me. She's smiling and her arms are stretched wide. And beside her there's Jesse, and Macy.

And holding hands between them is little Grace.

"You found her," I say, and everything is all perfect, just perfect, and everybody even looks just exactly like they are supposed to, and their hair is all gold and shiny in the sun.

About the Author

Dawn Renaud is a freelance writer, editor and writing coach in Penticton, B.C. Although all of the characters in this story are entirely fictional, the setting is very loosely based on the area where she grew up near Echo Lake on Creighton Valley Road, between Lumby and Cherryville.

24609861R00085

Made in the USA
Middletown, DE
01 October 2015